Land of Nod

and Other Stories

Land of Nod

and Other Stories

by Paul Green

1976
The University of
North Carolina Press
Chapel Hill

Copyright © 1928, 1946, 1949, 1963, 1976 by
Paul Green
All rights reserved
Manufactured in the United States of America
ISBN 0-8078-1269-2
Library of Congress Catalog Card Number 75-33880

Library of Congress Cataloging in Publication Data

Green, Paul, 1894–
Land of Nod, and other stories.

CONTENTS: Fine wagon.–Loud like thunder.–The cut tree. [etc.]
I. Title.
PZ3.G8248Lan   [PS3513.R452]   813'.5'2   75-33880
ISBN 0-8078-1269-2

Contents

For HUBERT *and* RUTH HEFFNER

Land of Nod
and Other Stories

Fine Wagon

The great forest rang as if with the clamor of iron bells from the belfries of the trees. Standing on the bank of the deep inky creek, Bobo strained with all his might at his fishing pole. Down in the depths somewhere a catfish big as a hog was hung on his hook and gradually pulling him in. Lower and lower bent the pole and inch by inch his bare feet slid in the slick mud. He felt himself jerked headlong toward the sickish black water, when there came a voice calling and a sudden soft breath blowing whiff in his ear. The great forest wheeled and turned over, rushed toward him, by him. The bells were silent, and in the wink of an eye the stream was gone and so were the fishing pole and the fish.

"Wake up, sonny, wake up—it's already day." And he felt a gentle hand diddling with his shoulder. —Who—what?— Mammy. But he must sleep, sleep a little more. And that fish— that great big fish!

"Wake up, sonny, your Pa's done fed the mules."

He grunted and squirmed about under the quilts and then sat up. Rubbing his scrawny dark fists in his eyes, he blinked at the little brown woman who stood by the bed holding a wiggling smoky lamp in her hand.

"Please, Mammy—please'm," he said. And then his eyelids dropped shut, he gaped and sank back slowly on the bed. Sweet sleepiness engulfed him instantly. Once more the edge of the great shadowy forest came moving toward him with its cool delicious shade, and once more he heard the lofty booming of the bells.

"Huh, so after all your proud bragging, you done forgot you're going with your pappy?" the voice said.

[3]

He heard the words afar off. They meant nothing to him, they were empty sounds. But only for a moment. Then remembrance flooded into him and he sat quickly up. Today was the day, and he was about to forget it. A sharp little rush of joy tickled somewhere in his chest behind his breastbone. He hopped out of bed as if a red-hot coal had been dropped inside his drawers. Cramming his shirttail down in his trousers, he followed his mother into the kitchen. He hesitated before the basin of waiting chilly water and then, roaching up his shoulders, soused his face down in his dipping cupped hands. "Whee—o—oo," he chattered. Already Mammy was at the stove taking the sweet fried fatback out of the pan. And now heavy brogan shoes came clomp-clomping along the porch, and Pappy entered —a tall grave black man.

"Morning, Bobo."

"Morning, Pappy," he answered, his scrubbed face coming out of the ragged bundle of towel.

"You done got that sleepy out'n them eyes—unh?"

"Yessuh, I'm all loud awake."

"That's a boy."

"When we going, Pappy?"

"Mmn—now not too big a swivet. We got to swallow a bite of grub first." And Pappy sat down to the table with his hat on, as he did when he had a pushing job ahead. Mammy hurried the corn bread from the stove and put it in front of him.

"Come on, Bobo," she said, but Bobo had already dived under her arm and onto his bench. She stood still at the end of the table with the dishcloth in her hand ready to get the coffee pot while Pappy bent his head over. "Make us thankful for what we're 'bout to receive," he mumbled, "and bless us all for time to come. Amen." "Amen," Bobo whispered fervently.

Nobody in the world could cook like Mammy. How good that fatback tasted, and the molasses and the bread! And then— what's that? He couldn't believe his eyes, as she came and set a cup of steaming coffee by his plate.

"Seeing how cold it is and you going off to work same like a man," she said.

His eyes were brimming with thanks as he poured his

saucer full of the dark stuff—dark as the water in that creek where the big fish stayed. Then he blew on it with a great oof the way Pappy did to cool it.

"Warm you up inside?" his father asked.

"It do that," he answered gulping it down with the noise of a small horse drinking water.

He gobbled his bread and meat, trying to keep up with Pappy, and in a few minutes breakfast was over. Mammy took Pappy's extra old coat from the wall and brought it to him.

"It'll be mighty cold riding out on that wagon, son," she said as she slipped it on him.

"Come on," said Pappy, and they hurried out of the house toward the barn. There in the grey morning light their fine wagon stood with its long tongue hanging out. It wasn't new like a white folks' wagon, but it was mighty nice just the same. He and Pappy had worked on it hard the day before, spiking up the loose spokes and driving wedges under the tires to tighten them for the heavy loads they'd have to haul. And with the new pine board seat laid across the body it stood waiting to ride.

Pappy had bought the wagon on credit at a sale a few days before for eight dollars. It would come in handy hauling stuff for the professors up in town, and in a week or two they would make enough to pay for it. After that they'd keep on hauling. Pappy had needed a wagon. When he came home a few weeks before, bringing old blind Mary to match with the other mule Suke, he had set his mind on something to hitch both of them to. He had traded a dog and a gun and two or three dollars for old Mary, and it would take a lot of hauling to get the money together to pay for the wagon. But shucks, Pappy was stepping on in the world, he was smart. Didn't Mammy say so yesterday at supper—that there weren't anybody smart like him. And she had kissed Pappy, feeling good about how things were going.

Last night Pappy had said, "Honey, I got me a job right off the bat. 'Fessor Haywood up there in town met me on the street today and said he had some wood to haul down where he's gonna build his chillun's swimming pool and could I haul it. 'Could I do it?' I says, 'Can't nobody do it better. I got me a fine wagon and a first-class team.' That's the way it goes in this world. You get ready for the job and the job gets ready for you. I says, 'I got a boy Bobo growing like a weed, and all muscling up. Me and him both'll be back heah tomorrow. Yessuh.'"

These things ran through Bobo's mind as he padded along toward the barn trying to keep up with his father's long stride.

"Yessuh, put me at a stick of wood and I'll tote my end," he said out loud.

"Huh, what's that?" Pappy asked, looking down at him but never slackening his pace.

"I mean—mean I'm gonna sure work hard."

And Pappy looked out toward the glad morning star, laughed a great laugh and patted him on the shoulder.

"How much that man gonna pay me, Pappy?" he inquired as they slid open the stable door.

"I bet a whole twenty-five cents, that's what you'd better charge him."

Twenty-five cents! And there'd be other twenty-five centses—nearly every day there would, for they would be so good at hauling that all the 'fessors would be asking them to do jobs. Twenty-five cents a day! His little skinny hand slid down into his pocket as if he already expected to find a piece of hard round money there. And once more, as had happened several times during the last day and night, the bright pictures of a new fishing hook and line gleamed for an instant in his mind. But he was cunning, he'd not mention that yet. But he knew where they could be got though. Up there in town in the hardware store—all with red corks and plenty of good lead sinkers.

"You try your stuff at bridling Suke," Pappy said, "this here new mule is kinder—er—mulish."

And pridefully Bobo opened the door and went in with the bridle in his hand. Old Suke stood with her head down as if expecting him, and slick as that old Syrian peddler, he put the bridle on her and led her from the stall. Then the business of harnessing and getting the bellyband and the hamestring tight. It didn't matter if Pappy did come around and retie the hame-string when he'd just managed to pull it together, for the hames were fitting snug in the collar and Pappy said that was doing fine as a fiddle.

"Them's stout hamestrings too," said Pappy. "Joe Ed let me cut 'em from that bull hide of his'n."

"I bet they'll hold—hold near 'bout a lion," Bobo spoke up.

"Or a' elevint," said Pappy. "Yeh, they'll hold—hold till the cows come home. And that britching, that's a real piece of scrimptious handiwork." And Pappy pridefully surveyed the old ragged strips of bedticking he had sewed together to help finish off the harness.

By this time the light of dawn had spread upward from the east across the sky, wide and spangled like a great peacock's tail, and Bobo wasn't afraid at all as he went into the loft and threw down two bundles of fodder for the mules' dinner. And now Mammy came out of the house bringing lunch wrapped up in a paper for her two menfolks. So everything was ready at last and not a bit too soon, for the smiling face of the sun was already peeping up over the edge of the world.

"You all be smart," Mammy called out as they climbed up into the wagon and sat down on the plank seat side by side. Pappy thudded his rope whip through the air with a great flourish, and off they went.

"We'll be home right around sundown!" he shouted back, "and me'n Bobo wants us a real bait of that fat side meat all fried and ready!"

"We'll be home at sundown!" Bobo repeated loudly, sticking his hand up out of his father's old coat sleeve in a little crooked gesture, half a wave and half a salute. He had seen the white boys on the college campus stick their hands up like that. And Mammy waved back at him, standing there by the gate with the new sun shining in her face.

They drove on down the dead-weeded lane and soon came into the high road. To the right and to the left stretched the sparkly frosty fields, and yonder in the distance the sun-fired church spires of the white man's university town stuck up above the wooded hill. The steel wagon tires made little harsh gritty sounds as they drove along.

"Don't this wagon run good, Bobo?"

"It sure do, Pappy."

"It orter—I was up and give it a good greasing whilst you was snoozing."

"You'd woke me up I'd been there and holp you."

"Them tiahs cries a little, but they's tight as a drum, ain't they?"

"Tight as Dick's hatband. We sure put the fixing on 'em, Pappy."

"Yeh, didn't we?"

"Get up there, Suke—you, Mary," Bobo chirped in his manful way. They were now mounting the hill, the air was sharp and biting, and Bobo had to clamp his jaws tight, his teeth were chattering so. But he'd never let Pappy know. They rode on in silence awhile. Bobo could see from Pappy's thoughtful face he was thinking of something. Maybe planning out the big work ahead and he didn't want to talk. A gang of robins flew across over his head going north. He watched them till they were little jumping eye-specks low in the sky. It would turn warm soon— today, tomorrow. It always turned warm after a heavy frost like this one. The robins knew—they were smart like people.

Soon they were rolling along the asphalt streets of the town, and for the moment Bobo feared the wagon wheels made too loud a sound. Every shop was closed, every place deserted. It was too early for the white folks to be up. They were different from colored folks who had to be out to get a soon start. Already some of the women cooks were on their way to work—their arms in front of them, their elbows gripped in the palm of each enclosing hand. It was cold and they walked in a hurry. Their shoes made a clock-clock on the hard sidewalks.

"Ain't everything quiet—like somebody asleep?" Bobo half whispered.

"Yeh," Pappy replied, "sleep. That's what's the matter with people, Bobo. They all sleep too much. Now look at you and me—we're up and doing."

"That's right," Bobo agreed soberly. And Pappy continued with feeling in his voice—"By the time other folks start to work we done done half a day. That's what gets a man ahead. He that rises 'fore the sun is the man what gets the most work done."

And now they were passing by the big grey granite bank building where the white men went in and out during the day, hauling in their money and putting it away. Bushels and bushels of yellow dollars and white dollars and bales of greenbacks they kept stored away there. That was where all the money came from to buy the things that people needed. That's where the money would come from to pay him and Pappy for their hauling. And to the left was the hardware store where they kept all kinds of blades, and knives and hooks—fish hooks. Well, when spring came again—.

Next down there by the drug store was the yellow and black sign of the telegraph office shut up and waiting. In a few hours it would be open, and folks would go in there and write things on a slip of paper, and a man would tap on a little handle, and them taps would be words that went out along wires and 'way to New York and maybe across the world through a pipe under the sea. Lord, Lord, weren't people smart! —Smart. But he was smart too, today he was.

Bobo had always been frightened by the big buildings and goings-on when he'd come up town to buy five cents worth of snuff or ten cents worth of fatback for Mammy and Pappy. But this morning he looked at the houses and stores with bolder eyes. He felt more at home among them today. He was a work-ingman now, and nobody ever bothered a workingman—not even big boys that liked to pick on you and throw your cap up and lodge it in a tree. He had something to do now, work for the white folks, and that made everything right. The white folks wouldn't allow any foolishness with any of their help.

In a few minutes they had gone through the village to the outer edge and came where a little alley turned off from the main street and down a hill into a new development.

"Is we 'bout got there yet, Pappy?"

"Yeh, right down yonder is where 'Fessor lives," and he pulled the heads of the mules into the alley. "He's got a lot of wood cut 'way down below his house there and he wants it hauled up to put in his cellar."

"Looks like a sort of rough place down there," Bobo said, straining his eyes ahead of him.

"Sure, but we're the men to get that wood up and out'n it, ain't we, Bobo?"

"Is that," Bobo spoke up strongly and briskly.

"And he's going to pay us a dollar a cord to move it. He said he had ten or twelve cords down there."

"How much is a cord, Pappy?"

And now they were turning off to the left down a little rock path that skirted around and away from the professor's house. What a house that was, all white and pretty, shining there among the bare trees! And how many chimneys did it have, and the windows with green blinds! Bobo almost caught his breath —there on the porch sat a big red bicycle. That must belong to one of the chillun, but he didn't mind how many bicycles the chillun had now 'cause some of these days he would—that too maybe—not a new one—no—no—just an old one.

"Well, a cord of wood is a pile 'bout ten feet long and as high as your head and you get a dollar for moving it," said Pappy. "Yeh, ten or twelve of 'em. I bet we near 'bout will move six or eight of them cords today, and that's six or eight dollars."

"Look out there, Pappy!"

"Sure," his father gravely replied as he pulled on the plowline reins and stopped the mules, for the wagon was going down the hill and almost pushing the collars up over their heads. "I better tighten up them britching strops a little bit," he said. Holding to the lines, he climbed down and scotched the wheel with a rock. In a few minutes he had tightened the straps of bedticking and got ready to go.

"You think you might drive some?"

"Lemme," Bobo answered eagerly.

Handing over the reins, Pappy got behind the wagon and held it back as the mules moved down the hill. What a strong man Pappy was, there pulling on the coupling pole like as if it had been the wagon's tail! And the mules had to push a little bit against the collar now that he was holding back so sharp.

They finally got safely down to the little wooded hollow where the firewood was piled in great heaps, and they did no damage at all other than tearing off a patch of bark from a sugar maple tree with the wagon hub. After much backing and sliding the rear end of the wagon around, by pushing and jerking on the coupling pole, they got set near a pile of wood and began to load it. It was a fine mixture of oak and pine cut in the proper lengths for the professor's fireplace, and Bobo liked to work at it, it looked so nice. Already he could feel how it would pop and burn, making a warm blaze to keep the chillun snug at night—there studying their books and playing with their toys. He heaved piece after piece up into the open wagon body trying to match his father. Talk about being smart—huh, with a few days of this stuff he'd put a muscle on his arm like a big mice running under his skin.

"All right," Pappy called, "try the end of that thing." And Bobo took hold of the big black log of solid hickory all ready to show his strength. Then they heard a heavy voice calling down from the house above, and looking up, Bobo saw a man wearing some kind of a gown standing by the porch railing with his hair all rumpled.

"Who's that?" Bobo asked, letting go of the log and stopping still as a post.

"S-sh, that's 'Fessor," Pappy said.

"Hey, what you doing down there?" the professor called. And Pappy even as far away as he was pulled off his hat quickly and bowed respectfully.

"Morning, 'Fessor," he answered in a low voice and smiled same as if 'Fessor was right in front of him.

"Morning, suh," Bobo whispered pulling off his hat likewise.

"You make enough racket to wake up the neighborhood," said the figure on the porch.

"Yessuh," Pappy began and then fumbled a bit for his words. "We thought we'd get an early start, suh."

"Well, you have that, it's just seven o'clock."

"Yessuh," and Pappy bowed again.

"Well, go on and be as quiet as possible. Haul the wood around to the cellar door. I'll come out a little later."

"Yessuh," said Pappy again, still holding his hat in his hand.

The figure on the porch looked around at the world,

yawned and retired into the house. Pappy and Bobo waited a moment and then went on with their loading but this time slow and careful-like, laying each piece of wood gently in the wagon as if they were packing eggs.

"Why do he do that?" Bobo at last timidly inquired.

"Who you mean do what?" his father asked in a low stern voice.

"The man up there in that big house—'Fessor."

Something seemed to be bothering Pappy, for he gripped the piece of wood motionless in his hand and looked at Bobo. "Why you ask that?"

"He kept looking around at the earf and up at the sky. It ain't going to snow, is it?"

"Oh," said Pappy as if he had been thinking of something else. And then he turned back to loading the wood again, and Bobo turned back also. But they decided to leave the big hickory log until the next load.

"Must be some kinder big man, ain't he," Bobo said presently, "living in that big house with all these woods around?"

"He's a 'fessor—teaches boys and gals. That's what 'fessor means." Pappy was silent a bit and then went on as if to himself, "He a mighty big man, and plenty of things to worry his mind. I heard some folks say he a big man," and now Pappy looked carefully about him.

"Huh?" said Bobo.

"Do what?" and Pappy seized a piece of oak and lifted it aloft.

"Yeh, do what, Pappy?"

"Don't ask so many questions. 'Fessor wants his wood hauled, he going to pay for it and we going to haul it. He a big man, he stands mighty high. I hear 'em say he writes books and play pieces and makes money enough—enough to burn." And surveying the pile of wood on the wagon, he added, "Looks like we 'bout got a load."

"What do he write about, Pappy?"

"Huh?"

" 'Fessor. Do he write tales like what Mammy read from a book that time?"

Pappy suddenly snickered and looked around at him in a way he didn't understand. Then he said, "Say he writes books and things about the colored folks."

"Sure?"

"Sure."

"And do the colored folks read 'em?"

"Shut your mouth and go 'way," Pappy answered. And snickering again, he went on, "White folks buy 'em and read 'em 'way off yonder. That's how he gets so much money to build his house and this here swimming pool."

Now Pappy's hand went into his pocket, and Bobo watched it like a hawk. How long had he been waiting for that! This time it was true, he was going to do it. And sure enough Pappy pulled out a twist of homemade tobacco and bit off a big chew. Bobo edged up to him, waiting. For a moment the twist hesitated in Pappy's hand, and then it pinched off a big crumb and handed it to him. Bobo's skinny black paw darted out and seized it quick as a bat catching a bug. He stuck it in his mouth, rolled it around with his tongue and settled it over on one side making his jaw stick out all manful-like.

"Well, reckon we better start up the hill with this," and Pappy gathered up the reins. Suke and Mary who had stood drooping in their tracks suddenly woke up as if a swarm of hornets had come up out of the ground at them. At Pappy's first word Suke gave a lunge forward and old blind Mary gave a lunge backward. "Get up there," he said, whopping Mary a blow on the rump with his whip. And now she sprang forward and Suke stood still. "You Suke!" he shouted. And quicker than hailing out of the sky the blows of the whip danced from one mule to the other. With a rattle and groaning of the wheels the heavy load began to move up the stony hill, and Pappy winked at Bobo as much as to say, "Ain't that pulling for you?"

As they swung around into the little road, the rear wheel hooked the sugar maple again. "Whoa," said Pappy, and just in time, for the coupling pole was bent like a sick cow's tail. The mules stopped, slumped in their tracks and began to gnaw the dead scattering brown oak leaves that hung from a branch above their heads. Suddenly the creaky twanging of a screen door opening sounded across the hollow. Bobo looked out toward the house and saw the professor partly dressed standing on the porch again.

"There he is again, Pappy," he said, clutching his father's arm.

"Whoa," said Pappy softly to the mules.

"Heigh," said the professor, "didn't I tell you to keep quiet down there?"

Pappy's hat was already off in his hands again as he answered gently, "Yessuh, yessuh, we're just getting started, 'Fessor, and we—" Pappy looked down at Bobo as if asking him what to say.

"Haven't you hung your wheel in that maple tree?" the professor called, and Bobo saw him sliding his suspenders on his shoulders in a quick nervous jerk.

"He's coming down here, Pappy," he whispered.

"No suh," answered Pappy, "we just giving the mules a little breathing space, suh!"

"Well, see that you don't hurt anything." And once more the professor gave his look around the world and turned back into the house.

After much prying and straining, they shoved the wheel loose from the tree, but not until another great gleaming gap of bark had been torn off in the process. When they had got the load further up the hill, they scotched the wheels and went back. Pappy grabbed up a handful of dirt, smeared it over the scars so that no one would notice them, and Bobo ran about picking up the pieces of bark which he hid under the fallen leaves. Then they returned to the wagon and rode out onto the high ground. They drove proudly around back of the house and stopped near the cellar door.

"Look a-there, Pappy," Bobo whispered horrified, pointing to one of the rear wheels. The wedges had fallen out from under the tire and the old wheel stood all twisted and crank-sided.

"Oh, that wheel'll stand up," said Pappy lightly, eyeing it. "We'll get unloaded and then take a rock and drive that tire back on." And climbing down, he wrapped the reins tight around a front wheel hub so the mules couldn't get at the spirea bushes.

Bobo passed the wood piece by piece to his father who took it in armfuls quietly down into the cellar. By this time the people in the house were astir, and Bobo could see into the kitchen where Miss Sally the cook, wearing some kind of fancy lace thing on her head, was preparing breakfast. The smell of coffee and bacon came out to him and he sniffed the air hungrily like a little dog. And now the professor reappeared, his face clean-shaven and his hair brushed. He came up to the wagon and looked sharply at the load. Bobo tried to keep his mind on his work handing down the wood to his father below, but he could smell the clear pine-winey stuff the professor had used for shaving. It filled the air, getting into his mouth and nostrils so wonderful and strong that he could taste it.

"You'll never move that wood with such a turnout as that," said the professor a little shortly and abruptly. "Look at that wheel!"

"Yessuh," answered Pappy, as he laid his hat on the ground beside him. "We'll fix that up in a minute, suh, the wedge just fell out."

"Yes, I see it did. How are you, son?" His voice was suddenly kind.

"Fine, thanky, suh," Bobo choked, almost speechless at being addressed by the mighty man who lived in such a house and had cooks and bicycles and automobiles and a big furnace thing down there in the cellar that kept the house warm.

"What's your name?" But now Bobo had lost his tongue.

"His name's Roosevelt, suh, but we calls him Bobo," answered Pappy gravely.

"H'm," said the professor softly. "And pile the wood straight back against the coal bin, will you?"

"Yessuh, we's fixing it up fine and dandy."

"And you can turn around down there next to the garage."

"Yessuh."

"What have you got in your mouth, son?" But Bobo could only stare at the professor with wide frightened eyes. "Don't you know chewing tobacco at your age will stunt you and keep you from growing up? Why, you're nothing but a baby." And once more the professor looked inquiringly about and up at the sky as he turned to reenter the house.

At last the load was stored away. And after much knocking and wedging down at the garage, the old wheel was strengthened, and they returned to the woods. But now it seemed the mules had decided not to do any more work that day. They kept twisting and turning about and sticking out their heads trying to get at the dead leaves. And when after a lot of trouble the wagon was finally backed and skewed around to another pile of wood, old Mary suddenly began to kick and lunge in the harness. Pappy seesawed on the reins and spanked her with the whip, and only after she had torn the britching off and burst one of his prized hamestrings did he finally get her quieted. All the while Bobo kept looking up toward the house expecting the professor to come charging out yelling at them. His heart was in his mouth, and he breathed again when at last the britching was mended, the hamestring retied and everything ready for the loading to begin. This time Pappy pitched the wood boldly into the wagon. The white folks were up and having breakfast, and the chatter of children was heard in the house. It didn't make any difference about noise now.

"We better not put such a heavy load on this time, had we, Pappy?"

"No, we ain't going to load up furder'n to the brim," he replied. And when they were ready once more, Pappy mounted briskly to the top of the seat and gave the word for the mules to go. Bobo started following behind, but old Mary acted like Satan was in her. She lunged forward, broke the hamestring again and ran straight out of the harness. And before Pappy could do a thing she had turned herself completely around and stood facing them with her white, sightless eyes as if laughing at them. Pappy lost his temper, and leaning far over with his rope whip, struck her a great knock in the face. She reared up on her hind feet, and giving a leaping jump, left the harness behind her.

"Look out, look out, Pappy!" Bobo squealed in fright.

Pappy sprang down from the wagon, and with a strong hold upon the reins kept old Mary from getting entirely loose and running away. Now from the porch Bobo heard the dreaded voice again.

"What is the matter down there!"

Bobo didn't dare look up, for he knew the professor was coming down the hill. And in a minute there his shiny black shoes stood beside them. Without a word Pappy dropped his whip on the ground and began straightening out the harness, and old Mary started greedily eating the dead leaves again. Suddenly the professor broke into a low laugh, and Bobo shook in his tracks. Somehow that laugh made him feel queer and trembly.

"Why in the name of mercy did you come trying to haul wood with such a mess as this?" the professor said.

"Yessuh, yessuh, but—" Pappy began.

"But nothing," the professor replied irritably and sharply, and he took a step backward and surveyed the wagon and the team. Then his voice was kind again. "Here, son, you hold her head and let's see what we can do." The professor took off his fine coat and undid his white collar and set to work tying up the britching and rehitching the traces on old Mary.

"You sure know your stuff 'bout mules, 'Fessor," Pappy broke in presently, standing there pinching a dead twig in pieces between his fingers.

"I was raised on a farm."

"Do tell, suh."

"And I learned not to starve a mule to death and not to try to haul wood with the harness and wagon falling to bits," he added.

Pappy was silent.

Bobo stood looking on, every now and then spitting in noiseless excitement off to one side. He watched the deft movements of the professor as if mesmerized, and now and then his gaze traveled to his father, who stood all shamed and humbled with his hat off. A queer lump rose up from his breast and stuck in his throat, and he swallowed quickly. Then he began sputtering, trying to get back the wad of tobacco that had gone down behind his breastbone. Gritting his teeth, he blinked and shook the tears out of his eyes, making little choking noises in his throat.

"What's the matter with you, son?" queried the professor, staring at him.

"Nothing," he answered quickly.

"You look sick. Have you had any breakfast?"

"Yessuh."

"Yessuh, we both et a big bait of good coffee and sidemeat 'fore we come off," Pappy said, coming over and timidly offering to help fasten the breast chains.

"You wait, I'll drive for you," said the professor a little sharply. And clucking kindly to the mules, he jiggled the reins gently. The wagon slowly began to move. The professor walked along as the mules pulled on up the hill, and then blam, that old rear wheel struck a stone hidden by the leaves, and with a moaning groan it collapsed. And now once more the professor gave his queer laugh. He stood a moment looking at the reins in his hand, and then throwing them down took out some money and handed it to Pappy. "Here's a dollar, though you've not earned fifty cents," he said.

"Thanky suh, thanky suh," said Pappy, wiping his hand on his coat and humbly taking the money.

Without a word the professor turned and strode off toward the house. When he had gone a little distance, he turned and called, "Take your bundle of trash and clear out. I'll get somebody else to haul my wood! I'm sorry." With that he was gone.

Bobo stood looking at the ground. He could see the toes of his father's ragged shoes in front of him. Finally the shoes moved, and he heard his father say, "I reckon we just about as well quit and go home, son." And then he heard another voice saying—a woman's voice up on the porch—"What's the matter, honey?" and the professor replying, "The same old story—My God, these everlasting Negroes—poverty—trifling! Come on, let's finish our breakfast." And the door of the great house slammed shut like the jaws of a steel trap.

Pappy slowly began unloading the wood and laying it gently and heavily on the ground. All the while Bobo stood by without moving. His hands and arms hung down by his sides. He made no effort to help Pappy or do anything, but just stood there. "Come on, boy," Pappy said harshly.

When they had finished unloading, Pappy tied a limb to the coupling pole under the axle, and the old broken wheel was loaded into the wagon body. Then they climbed up onto the seat. And the mules now as if glad to be free of work moved quickly up the hill and back into the main highway. Through the town they rode, the old limb dragging under the wheel-less end of the axle. People looked out from the houses as they passed, and a group of white school children playing tag on the sidewalk stopped and pointed at them. Bobo sat on the seat by Pappy looking straight ahead, and Pappy was looking straight ahead too. When they neared the business section of the village, Pappy turned off and went along a side street. And soon they came to the other edge of the town and descended the hill.

When they rode up near the yard gate, Mammy unbent from her sweeping by the door and stared at them.

"Why you back so early?" she called. "I ain't got a speck of dinner ready. Eyh, and look what's happened to your wagon wheel!"

"Shet your mouth, woman!" Pappy roared.

Jumping down from his seat, Bobo entered the yard.

"We don't want no dinner," he heard his father's rough brutal voice shout behind him.

"What's the matter, son?" Mammy said.

"Nothing, nothing," he gulped. And catching hold of her apron, he began to sob.

"Dry up!" Pappy yelled after him, but Bobo sobbed and sobbed.

"What's happened, son?" Mammy said, smoothing his woolly head with her hand.

"Nothing, nothing," he spluttered.

And then a dreadful thumping and squealing began in the edge of the yard. But Bobo didn't look up. There was no need to. For even with his face buried in his mother's apron and his eyes stuck shut with tears, he could see a skinny black man there by the woodpile beating old Mary with an ax-helve, and that black man was Pappy—and he was ragged and pitiful and weak.

Loud Like Thunder

*B*obo *whirled away* and ran across the yard toward the house. His mother reached out her arms to take him in, but he sidestepped her like a football player skeeting along a broken field, and on around behind the house he fled.

He turned helplessly about, looked around at the earth and up at the cloudless overarching sky. He went over and plopped down on the back steps with his chin caught fiercely in his hand. The jerking of his shoulders gradually subsided, his eyes stopped their wet and hot blinking, and finally he began staring steadily out before him. The front and back doors of the cabin were open now that the sun had warmed things up, and he could see through the house to a patch of light in the yard where Pappy and Mammy were. And Mammy was talking in pleading, soothing tones.

"Please, honey, don't let it worry you so," she was saying. "Never mind, never mind—don't."

And Pappy was answering back angrily and brutally, "That's the way it is, gal, that's the way!" His anguished voice was breaking in the air. "And I keep thinking, and I keep thinking—" The voice died out, faded, and rumbled away down deep in the caverns of his breast.

Bobo put his hands over his face, then peeped sideways between his spread-out fingers and kept on staring through the house. Pappy was sitting on the wagon tongue, his shoulders bent over, and Mammy was standing by him, hugging his face against her the way she had been hugging his own self a few minutes before. Old Mary and Suke were free from the wagon and at peace as if nothing had happened and were nibbling and grabbing at the dead grass along the edge of the little lane. Now Pappy pulled his head up and looked off, his great gnarled hands gesticulating and shaking in the air. And Bobo could see as plain as if they were in three inches of his face those great knotted veins that stood out on his hands.

"The way that white man look at me, 'bused me—ah!" Pappy blazed out suddenly.

"Don't cry, baby, don't," Mammy was begging.

"What good do it do to try—and I try hard," he went on brokenly. "They put out the light, make the day dark like a cloud and the sun go down. They stomp on me, squash me. I'm a fool, that's what! And they ain't no hope—"

"Honey, honey," Mammy implored.

But he wouldn't stop. "Never no hope. They put a fence 'round the world and shut me out, put up palings to divide me. Today I was gonna get started—be on my way—now look! Look! I'm at the bottom, girl, and gonna stay at the bottom." And he stood up, pulling Mammy's arms away from him. But no sooner had he done so than they were back around him again, like wild vines to their clinging, and she was gazing piteously up in his dark, working, wretched face.

"Don't look like that, honey. Your poor eyes!" Her voice was half-weeping now. "I got my arms about you, all safe, honey. I hold you tight. We stick together, we keep on sticking together, and we'll make it, somehow we'll make it."

Bobo closed his fingers tight over his eyes. He couldn't see any more. He didn't want to hear any more. He felt the gush of sobs breaking and tumbling in him, struggling to pour out through his lips. Never had he heard Pappy's voice sound like that, never had he heard a grown-up man talk like that. And then he heard the voice again, saying, "I ain't no 'count, got no manhood. If I had I'd get me a gun and go up there and—" Bobo crammed his fists into his ears, sprang up and hurried off across the back yard by the pigpen and on toward the waiting, quiet woods there beyond the fields.

He wandered lonesomely about. He couldn't sit still, he couldn't stand still. The golden sun shone luminously over the great sweet gums, the white-bellied sycamores, and the glistening hollies. But now he felt the chill of evening already permeating the twiggy bare branches with its icy stillness. And though the sky was cloudless, it seemed to him slaty and cold and biting and threatening a freezing sleet.

Finally he sat down on a rotting pine log where the spring before he had pried off the sappy bark hunting for flatheads to fish with. And there he sat, his head bent over, motionless in his grief.

Soon the sounds of the woods that had quieted at his approach resumed. A sapsucker on a nearby sugar maple began giving his meticulous and stern staccato rapping again, and a few snowbirds hopped springily about on the ground, rustling and overturning dead holly leaves. And a shy towhee jumped and flit-fluttered merrily in and out of a brier thicket. Somewhere far away in the top of a dead pine a yellowhammer gave his piercing boyish call, and deep in the woods along the branch behind him Bobo heard the shy fluffy brown partridges making their furtive clucking as they gathered under a dark cedar to roost. But he paid no attention to any of these familiar and beloved sounds of other days.

Suddenly an overpowering hunger came upon him, not for food or ice cream or goodies but for tobacco. A taste for it was in his mouth and throat, a fierce compelling hunger. He reached out and tore off a headed twig from a toothbrush tree and began avidly chewing on it.

Mammy's voice shrilled down across the field from the house. "Bobo! Bobo!" it called. "Come get yo'self some'p'n t'eat."

He continued to sit there, thinking, and made no answer. Sometime later he heard a rhythmic, rasping beating sound out in the fields. Looking up, he saw Pappy slowly moving along between the cotton rows, flailing down the dead stalks for spring plowing. He wasn't able to own a stalk-cutter and so the tough half of a broken shovel-handle must do instead for a flail.

Bobo watched him working there. His strong long arm

showered down in dogged blows upon the upright stalks. Every winter as long as he could remember Pappy had beaten down the stalks, working, working away. Yes, that was it, work.

"He works hard, I tell you." And his voice broke the stillness as if he were arguing with someone. He sprang up from the log and began looking around him in the woods. Presently he found a tough hickory limb and finally broke it off from the sprawled dead top of the tree which had been cut down the winter before for wood. He stamped the small branches from it, went out into the field and sturdily began to work. Pappy paid no mind to him, not even so much as the flicker of an eye, but went on with his rhythmic and primitive beating, right and left, left and right, his feet moving steadily and slowly forward. Pappy soon outdistanced him, but Bobo kept on working. The upper outside muscles of his arm began to ache and presently were paining him like a sore tooth. His wrist grew weak and almost limp, but he gritted his teeth and flailed away at the endless and increasingly tough stalks.

When nightfall began to darken the fields, Pappy laid his stick aside at the end of the row and went on toward the house, his shoulders and head leaning a bit forward as if cresting against the coming darkness as he went. Bobo long before had begun switching his stick from one hand to the other to ease his aches. Now taking both hands to the stick and pushing up his energy, he flailed the stalks loudly to attract Pappy's attention so that he would turn and call to him to come on to the house. But Pappy never looked around. On by the house he went and toward the barn with never a turn of his head.

The night came on down and Bobo's hands by now were blistered and almost bleeding. He was near to sobbing too. He glanced fearfully toward the swamps where such ghosts as the Iron-faced Man and the little Willy-wisp Girl lived. He beat his way on blindly out to the end of the row, dropped his stick, and stepped painfully toward the house.

Mammy tried her best to be cheerful at supper. But after a little talk about the weather and how according to the old saying, the 'tater bugs ought to be fewer next year 'cause of the early freeze they had had, she too gave it up and ate away quietly. Pappy drank several cups of black coffee, fumbled with his bread and meat, then got up and went and sat by the fire. He took his shoes off and rocked back and forth, chewing his tobacco. All the while Bobo ate his unwanted supper as best he could.

He left the table and went and sat down in front of the fire. But unlike his father he had no tobacco to put into his mouth. Nor did Pappy make any motion to offer him any as he usually did. Mammy now was busy in the back room fixing the beds extra for the especially cold night. He got up to go into the room where she was.

"Where you going, boy?" Pappy called out roughly. He turned, came back and sat down. For a while he stared at the fire waiting for Pappy to continue. Presently he did. His voice was cold, crisp, and businesslike. "I've decided," he said, "we can't make nothing at this hauling business and we're going back with Graham Love and Kluttzy Trice again to cut crossties tomorrow."

"But—" Bobo started to say, then gulped and stopped.

"No but about it," Pappy spoke up in a voice that allowed no argument. "That doctor didn't know what he was talking about. And what difference do it make if he did!" He struck his breast a resounding blow with the flat of his hand. "And there won't be no schooling for you this year—before Christmas nor after Christmas—and maybe none next year neither." He spat sharply toward the fire, chewed on in silence a while and then concluded, "Go on to bed now, you need your sleep. We got to get a soon start in the morning."

Bobo rose and went into the bedroom. Soon he was undressed down to his long underwear, and he crawled into his narrow cold bed. Mammy came over and pulled the cover up around his shoulders. He reached out and grabbed her hand fiercely in his, holding it and smoothing it against his face. "Poor Mammy," he said.

She peered down at him, then tweaked his nose. "Poor nothing! What's come over you, boy? Forget all that foolishness. Tomorrow's another day."

"Sing me that song, Mammy," he said.

"Pshaw, chile, you ain't no baby no more," she said.

"Sing it, Mammy."
She sat down on his bed and began.

"Oh where you going, lord angel,
  Your wings all dipped in gol'?
I'm bound for the River Jordan
  To rest my weary soul."

Pappy's voice called from the other room, "Come in here, gal."

She stood quickly up. "Go right to sleep," she whispered. "I got to talk to your pappy."

She hurried out of the room and closed the door behind her. For a long while he could hear the two of them in there talking in low tones. At last he drifted off to sleep, a wide, vast, dreamless sleep.

Sometime later he awoke. The shrunk moon had risen and now shone through the window in a vague and pallid mistiness. At first he thought it was daybreak. Then he knew from the way the light fell by the chair and across the floor that it was the good old moon high in the middle of the sky. He listened for his father's snore. He heard his mother's deeper breathing, but not his father's. He softly reared himself up on his elbow and looked around, but only the lumpy outline of Mammy showed in the double bed against the wall. A vague unhappiness and misery were in him. Then it was that the day's experience came back to him, the full knowledge of the blasting of his and Pappy's dreams—of schooling, a new suit for Christmas, and a cook-stove which Mammy'd been praying for so long.

"Mammy," he called softly. But his mother's soft, deep breathing continued. Through the moonlight another light glanced and glimmered suddenly on the window pane, and he saw a big low star across the cotton patch out toward the barn. Big as a magnolia flower it was. Then the star blacked out and reappeared again. He sat up on the edge of his bed watching it. It showed itself once more and stood steadily burning, right in the middle of where the barn should be. For an instant there

surged in his mind one of the wild stories told by his grand-
mother about how her mammy had seen the stars fall on the
world, how some of them lodged in trees and hung there,
sizzling and burning, and shooting sparks and brimstone into
the air, and all the wicked people had confessed their sins and
joined the church from the fear of the judgment day. Then he
realized that it was not a star but Pappy's lantern. He was out at
the barn for some reason or other.

"Mammy, where's Pappy?" he called again.

He waited but there was no answer. Something was wrong
with Pappy or he wouldn't be out there, and the night already on
toward morning.

He slipped quietly out of bed, pulled on his clothes and
shoes and crept from the room. Crossing the yard, he saw that
the light was in a stable now. He went on into the barn lot, and
through the open stable door he saw a queer sight. There Pappy
was working around old Mary. He had a bucket of water and a
big rag and was bathing the mule's wounds and welts where he
had beaten her with the ax-helve. The wad of hardness which
had been lodged in the boy's breast so long suddenly began to
melt and all thinking with it. He must have made a little whimpering sound, for Pappy looked out dully and blinked in his
direction. "What you doing there—boy?" he called. The next
moment he ran out of the darkness toward Pappy. "Great God!"
Pappy spoke up sharply, as he jerked his head around.

"Let me help you, Pappy. Lemme."

"You scared me same as a ha'nt. Get on back to bed."

"I want to help you, Pappy," he insisted brokenly. He held
out his hand. Pappy looked at him for a long moment and then
without a word tore off a piece of the big rag and handed it to
him. And the two of them went on bathing old Mary's wounds.

"That'll teach her a lesson, all right," Bobo spoke up presently and encouragingly. Pappy said nothing. "She deserved a
beating, the way she misbehaved. And she's going to be all
right, Pappy. She will."

"Yeh," said Pappy. And then he added, "She's a good
mule."

And when they'd wrung out the rags and dried off the

hurt places, Pappy dipped out axle-grease he'd bought for his wagon and spread it over the sores with a flat little paddle.

"That'll cyore her up fine," said Bobo.

"Yeh," said Pappy.

"Sho'," he murmured. "Tomorrow she won't know it."

"I want her to get well soon," said Pappy. "I'm going to sell her off and the wagon too. We don't need her."

"No, we don't need her," he said, "nor the wagon."

They were finished. Pappy stood looking at the mule. Abstractedly he picked up the lantern. But still he stood without moving. Bobo looked at him questioningly. Reaching out he touched his arm. "We better get back to the house, Pappy. It's mighty cold on you."

"Boy," said Pappy finally, and he didn't look down at his son. He stared off at a corner of the stable, "I want you to remember this day."

"Yessuh," Bobo said in a low muffled voice. He made a motion as if to start toward the house, but Pappy still stood as he was.

"Remember this day," he went on.

"Don't, Pappy," he whispered.

Now the father looked down at his son and his eyes were bright and stern. "You done seen what it is to be a poor ignorant nigger. Hear me!" And turning, he strode out of the stable, forgetting to close the door. So fast he went that the cobwebs hanging down from a crack in the loft swayed in the wind. Bobo stood watching him go.

And loud like thunder he had heard him.

The Cut Tree

Day after day now Purdie Banks and Bobo worked hard in the woods, cutting the post oak and the white oak trees and hewing them out in their flattened eight-foot links for crossties. Up early and stay late—chop, chop, chop, whack, whack, whack, whee, wheeah, whee—with ax and adz and crosscut saw. And now and then Bobo's flaring imagination wandered as he worked. He would think of the time when the great trains would be running on the rails from the North to the South and from the East to the West over these same crossties that his hands were helping to shape. The rich and the poor would ride upon them, and the weak and the powerful, the white and the colored. And maybe some Indian redmen likewise and their mighty chief would ride, all with their feathers and tomahawks. And who knows, maybe kings and queens would ride too and the 'way up high president of the country itself. And in rain and wind and hail and the foggy dark the great trains would be blowing whoo-whoo as they thundered along, his own handiwork helping to hold them up as they fled forever onward, with their huge fiery eye lighting the fearful way ahead.

And in his scattered thinking and in the great fervor of chopping and hacking, something of the grief and nameless hurt that had been his of late eased itself away and settled like the dregs of a quieting ferment into a residue at the bottom of his being—waiting a far-off hour perhaps when a storm of passion might stir them up again. He was already more sober and thoughtful. And gone were his wild elation and childish joy of former days—gone for a while.

Graham Love would look out at him and say, "You sho' is mighty quiet for a boy. What's on your mind, son?"

"Nothing," Bobo would answer.

But now and then there were spurts of the old joy in him. And how excited he got at the mighty crashing and booming of the bare-limbed white oak trees as they struck against the earth! Sometimes too he felt sorry for these big fellows, they were so helpless as they wavered and gently swayed and then with a tearing cracking of their white entrails came toppling down in a whooshing moan to slap their tops against the ground. And how he liked to hear the wheeah—wheeah of the crosscut saw on frosty mornings! And he loved to see Graham Love and Kluttzy Trice drive their sharp five-pound Black Kelly axes deep into the white flesh of these trusting silent creatures of the woods. He was proud too to learn how to sharpen the axes and the adzes. Kluttzy Trice taught him that. He would take the whetstone of petrified rock, spit manfully on it, and put a razor edge on the tools during the lunch hour while the men sat about in the warm splotches of the winter sun and took their rest among the beat-down huckleberry and Indian wild currant bushes. And he grew clever at working on the big teeth of the crosscut saw with a file, bringing them to a gleaming jagged sharpness.

But there was always that strange and nameless ache waiting within him, that sense of something wrong with the world. He would look at the great muscled bare arms and leather-braceleted wrists of Graham and Kluttzy as they swung their axes, and yet they were not the strong men they seemed to be. Not quite. He would listen to their bragging stories of bone and brawn, how they had pulled this or that mighty man down knee-deep into the earth with the handspike at logrollings, or how they had whipped a certain bull of the woods in fist and skull combat, how much money they had earned in their time and what they could buy now if they had kept it all, how many women had loved them and cooked for them and borne them children, and other boastful things. And they would cut their eye at him for his look of childish and fervent admiration, but instead they would most often meet a look of rather cool and grave disapproval or skeptical disbelief.

And then he would glance across at his father's gaunt whiplash form and speak up. "We'd better get back to work. But you rest up some mo', Pappy."

"Listen at that boy," Graham said. "Just plumb smart as he can be."

"A new ax cuts clean—till it gets dull," said Kluttzy.

"And a gap in the blade shows in the chips," Graham opined laconically.

"Yeh, we'd better get back to work," said Purdie. And his coughing broke out again.

And through the rain and sleet of January and through the dark bitter gusts of February weather, Purdie and Bobo hacked and sawed and labored on—to pay themselves out of debt and to buy food and clothes for the family. And every Saturday afternoon they loaded up the teams sent into the woods by Mr. Merritt. They would receive their twenty-four cents—cash or credit—for each of the eight-foot crossties they'd cut, and stagger home to rest on Sunday. Persistently, stolidly, Purdie kept at it, and just as persistently Bobo helped him. But Purdie's strength was seeping away in the tear and strain of his muscles and the turmoil of his frustrated mind. Bobo now and then would speak to Pappy—fatherlike and authoritative, and in a strange way somewhat aloof withal.

"You got to rest, Pappy."

"They ain't no rest," Purdie would snap back.

"Remember what Doctor Hargraves said."

"Yeh, and he don't know," Purdie would retort angrily. "And if he did know what difference do it make?"

As time had gone on, fewer and fewer words except snapping and irritated ones came out of Purdie's lips. At night the two would eat their supper and fall into bed, Bobo to sleep as sound as a tick from exhaustion. But his father would often toss and turn all night with the rupturing riving cough which now beset him and shook him to his feet even as a sudden whirlwind shakes and makes totter a loosening dying pine in the forest.

Mammy prayed and hoped for the spring to come soon, for then Purdie would get better. The mulligrubs of winter would fade away and the warm sunlight would drive the germs out of his festering lungs. And in the hot fiery July heat the phlegm and rheum of the damp caverns of his breast would be dried up and he would breathe easy and be well again. She thought so, she said so again and again, and she prayed so.

Then March came, and one of those false and warm sun-filled days of spring. Blissful sunshine poured down upon the earth, and the bees and butterflies made whoopee and sped wildly about, merry little sprites in the sunbeamed air. The young dirt daubers and wasps pushed forth from their cells and tried their wet wings in the drying sun, falling or tumbling here and there and hanging on blades of grass like tender helpless teeny fledglings, then climbing up to try again. The bluebirds went thirra-lu-eeing in the elms and catalpa trees around the house, sailing from limb to limb, full of the urge and leapings of spring. And ever the wind blew soft over the land.

That day Bobo and Purdie went more happily into the woods. The gentle wind that caressed their faces rolled and lifted great billowy clouds like white-winged sailing ships out of the southwest over and across the sky, to pile them up on the eastern horizon, and now and then a little footloose whirlwind came out of nowhere and gurgled its glee among the twigs and branches of the bare trees as it sped on, rocking the tall tops of the spiky sweet gums for a moment and reminding Bobo of the time he had seen some old drunken colored women dancing and swaying and cutting up behind Mr. Eubanks's store there by the University campus.

Yes, winter was over. All threat of snow was gone. The chirping bluebirds, the whistling redbirds, and the hopping alert robins playing about, exploring and hunting for places to build their nests proved it so. And the turtledoves sat in the road in two's, all gentle, making their quiet but passionate love. The rain crows, those shy yellow-billed cuckoos, gave their vacuous hollow call or their wooden scraping cluck from the depths of the forest. And the tireless bee-martins and swallows dipped and soared and even stray bullbats were seen skittering and diving with their vulgar bowel-splattered brayings across the sunset sky.

Aye, in no time at all sweet April would be here, sap

would flow up soon now through the bodies of all the oak trees, and crosstie cutting would be finished until the cold weather of the coming fall had shrunk the life juice downward and hardened the wood again.

All the morning as they worked Purdie had seemed more cheerful. He even talked to Bobo about getting out the old Boy Dixie plow, putting a new point on it and borrowing one of Mr. Merritt's mules to hitch with Suke and beginning to two-horse break land again. Old Mary had already been sold off or rather given away for he only got four dollars for her and three for the wagon. This year he would plant a few more acres of cotton and corn than usual and maybe a couple of acres of tobacco. Yes, he had to make things hum this year. And certainly then Bobo would be able to get some schooling.

Then about noon a change took place in the weather as so often happens in Carolina when winter is on the point of leaving and spring is coming in. More times than not this old winter will give a final tussle before he will yield over to warm weather. Sometimes it will seem as if out of revenge he will lie low for a few days like a cunning marauder. The sun will shine brightly and warm even as now. The poor foolish domestic plum trees, peach and pear trees, and even the wise wild trees in the woods, such as the red oak, the redbud, the willow, the buckeye, the ancient white hickory, and the hard dogwood will begin to put forth their buds and sprouts. And all the while old winter keeps lying low like Br'er Fox in the story, watching and waiting.

Then seemingly when these innocents have trustingly opened their tender greenery to the sky he shakes himself like a great bear and comes roaring and blowing his breath out of the north, from far beyond Hillsborough, across the Eno River, across New Hope Creek and across Morgan's Creek and Purefoy's millpond, chilling and sheeting them all with his icy breath and wrinkling the frozen ground as hard as an old ram's horn. And behind him as he sweeps on he leaves the sky overcast with a murky yeastiness of clouds. Soon these clouds begin to spit a bit of sleet and snow and then send it pelting down, and the poor already budding flowers and trees are swiftly blistered and shriveled unto death.

Purdie and Bobo had gone carelessly off to work that day without overcoat or coat. They should have known better. Purdie especially, for he had lived through nearly forty changing and treacherous winters. And when at noon the wind began to whip around and a chilliness filled the air with a gloomy gustiness and the sky started fermenting, they had nothing with which to protect themselves from the wintry weather and they knew they were in for it. The wind stirred and shifted and whoomed about from the southwest to the west, then to the northwest and finally to the north itself, where it settled into a steady blowing of frosty breath as if from the cavernous mouth of some unseen giant of cold or that northern bear spoken of hid there far beyond the world's rim.

The billowy friendly clouds turned to cold smeary rainy ones, now suddenly discharging aimed and venomous showers of cold water drops and hail on the two helpless workers. Graham Love and Kluttzy Trice had brought their overcoats, and for once Bobo had to acknowledge to himself that they were smarter than he and his father.

Soon the two were drenched and chilled to the bone. And though they hurried the several miles home as fast as they could, Purdie's teeth were chattering and his lips were ashy and blue-wizened before they got there. Katie hustled up warm dry clothes for him, popped him into bed, and placed jars of hot water around him. But his teeth kept chattering and the bed shook and creaked from his bad chill as if the house were caught in a tremor of earthquakes.

Next morning he was burning up with fever. Bobo was none the worse for the wetting except that he had to keep wiping his running nose with his now shiny snot-hardened coatsleeve. The anguished and loving Katie said she'd have to go get her mother but Purdie said no. He wanted her to bring the herb women. They could cure him. "Don't bother Ma Althy," he said. "Don't bother her."

So Katie went across the field and got old Izilla and Lessie Trice, Kluttzy's ancient sisters. They came bringing a big jug of their herb juice—a brew made out of boiled wild cherry bark, sassafras roots, and mullein leaves and seasoned with honey.

[33]

The three women dosed Purdie thoroughly with it. And all the while Bobo was helping them like the good little nurse he was.

"Ums'll pyearten right up now," said old Izilla. "It brung Muh when um's had it."

"Ums'll be better right off," intoned old Lessie. But the next day Purdie was worse. They gave him more of the brew, but it did no good, and on into the next day and night. By this time he was turning and rolling in his bed, babbling incoherently and with his great liquid brown eyes, sick-glazed and weary, staring and turning aimlessly in their sockets. And most of the time Katie and now Graham Love or Kluttzy Trice, Purdie's partners, sat in the sickroom. Shadrack Foushee, a neighbor from across the creek, came, stayed awhile, and went away. And Bobo sat there too, his soul caught in dread and anguish and shrunken small within him. He couldn't leave. His heart ached and ached with a pain which he felt right up into the base of his throat and the back of his neck, some nameless strange pulling of pity and sorrow for his father who was suffering so.

And hour after hour he sat near the bed silent in his chair. There was in him some queer unspoken lamentation, a kind of wordless grieving over some lack, some frustration, some opportunity which he'd always known his father would rise to meet, and good luck and good things would come to him. But just now with his own ears he had heard old Izilla say there was little that could be done. And everybody knew that she was a good and smart old woman. Still she wasn't a white person and maybe she was wrong.

But then, there was that deathly look on his father's face. A look he had never seen before. Yes, once he had seen it, just a glimpse of it, and it was gone—the day at the professor's house when Professor Haywood handed him a dollar and said, "You've not earned fifty cents." But the look went away then. It quickly went away. But now the sick dead look didn't go away, it stayed there.

Yes, it was true, something awful was going to happen to Pappy. It was happening right now.

And the weeping of his mother Katie, the shaking of her

shoulders, the solemn grieving faces of Graham Love and Kluttzy Trice, and of the two herb women—all seemed to betoken the presence of some awful Something in this house. Yes, it was death in this house. These signs, these facts, crushed Bobo with their certainty. And all the hopes his father had had and all the hard work, the long talks they'd had together, the plans they'd made in the fields and in the woods for farming and for his own schooling—everything was coming down to nothing now.

"You've got to go to bed," Katie kept telling Bobo whimperingly. But he said never a word, sitting there straight in his hickory-bottomed chair, the chair that he had so often pushed forward for his father to sit in and warm his great hands by the fire.

"Let him be," said Graham Love. "Death is a thing you got to get acquainted with." And Kluttzy quoted one of his old sayings—

> *"Get used to a thing when young*
> *You'll stand it when you're old."*

Even in his grieving it occurred to Bobo how wrong they were. Death was something nobody ever could get used to. He knew he'd never be able to stand it. Death was the most terrible and horrible thing in all the world. Near daybreak of the fourth night he was awakened from a dream in his bed by Mammy Katie's loud voice wailing out a spill of high-crying and wordy lamentation, "Purdie, precious love, Purdie, Purdie!"

He opened his eyes and jerked up his head as a stiffening fear ran from his shoulders into his biceps and down his back and under his crotch.

Once more he had been dreaming, but not about the great fish in the creek. Strangely he had not dreamed that dream for a long time, not since the night before he and Pappy had got up early to haul wood for the professor. In this present dream he was cutting a great oak tree down for crossties, his ax sinking deep into its white pale heart at every blow, deeper than even

Graham Love could sink it. And from the air he could hear the voices of the colored school children, not mocking this time but bragging on him. Though he couldn't see them, still he could hear them, hear them singing and chanting, "Smart, smart, Bobo's smart. And look how strong he is." And then came the tottering of the great giant, and its leafy top leaning across the sky, the cracking of the breaking heartwood fibers in the gash, and then the almost sudden self-propelled hurtling of its body downward, and with a great suction of wind to follow. And just as it fell violently toward the earth there he saw his own self standing beneath it. With a shriek in his dream he had cried out but it was too late. The tree crushed down on him, the great leafy foliage smothering over him. Although the time for cutting crossties was wintertime, still in his dream the great tree was leafy and green. "Pappy, Pappy!" he had cried in a terror of supplication, "help me! help me!"

But it was Mammy's voice speaking his father's name now as he woke up, and there she and Graham were trying to hold Purdie down in the bed. And he was thrashing his arms about and babbling wildly, "Out of the way, you all folkses, out of my way. Yes, sir, Captain, yes sir, coming right up, coming right up."

"Purdie, Purdie," wailed Katie. "You got to lie down."

"You're a bad boy, Purdie," Graham said sternly. "Behave yourself." And he pushed the dying man back onto his pillow. But he bounded up again moaning and babbling and furiously flinging his arms about. In his delirium he was back on a job he had held a few years before as a day laborer carrying brick up for the University's new library building.

Graham and Kluttzy helped hold Purdie on the bed again, and then presently he spoke out in his normal voice. It was as if his brain had suddenly cleared. "Bobo," he called softly, "where you, son?"

"Here I am, Pappy," said Bobo quickly as he stood by the bed. One of his father's great gaunt hands came out and grabbed his smaller one and held it tightly, rubbing it spasmodically and furiously against his own burning beardy cheek.

"Bobo, where are you, Bobo?" he repeated.

"I'm right here, right here close beside you, Pappy," he quavered.

For an instant the sick man's eyes unclouded, and the conscious reason which was the self of Purdie Banks looked through.

"I hear you, boy, I hear you," he said. "Listen to me. Plenty times I tell you to hear me, boy. This is the last time and you got to listen. You be the head of the house now, take care of your mammy, hear me."

"Yes sir, yes sir, Pappy."

"Head of the house—you got to be the man—not like me. Got to be—maybe—something—got to get schooling—learn your books—things will come your way. Be a good boy. I tried but couldn't make it."

And then the light of understanding died out of his father's eyes as the black senseless surge of death flooded through his being. Purdie shrieked and started up again. "Coming right up, Captain, coming right up!" And then he spoke quietly, "Yessuh, 'Fessor, be right there bright and early. Giddup Mary, you, Suke."

And now the world and all its tokens and beloved objects perished from him. The last influx of oxygen was consumed in his blood to light the lamp of his life. His breath was suddenly sucked out of him and his strength cut instantly off as the struggling engine of his heart gave its last pumping beat.

Thirty-nine years ago this heart had started its first stirring and had never ceased once till now. He gasped, crumpled nervelessly down in bed, his head falling almost on his stomach. He rolled over on his side. A great shuddering shaking passed through him. The air compressed itself out of his lungs in a tiny long-drawn sigh much like the sound made by a subsiding mechanical doll or bellows when dropped by the careless hand that formerly moved it.

"It's over," Graham said.

"Pappy's dead." A whisper of horror broke from Bobo's lips. A moment he stood staring at his father's motionless form

—lying there dead as a fallen tree. Katie began to fill the room with shrieks. Bobo turned and ran blindly out of the house and down across the field into the waiting, sheltering woods. There he sat on a log, lost in an immensity of pain while his tears drip-dropped on the dead leaves at his feet and the dawn-wakened birds chattered and pshawed volubly in the trees above him. Long, long he sat there motionless, cold, and unutterably alone.

Bright Sparkles
in the Churchyard

*I*t *was a balmy day* in spring and a funeral was going on in the
Negro section of the cemetery close by the University wall. And
there before the open grave amid her neighbors stood a thin
middle-aged mulatto woman, mother of the dead young man
who was to be buried, there by an unmarked grave, his father's.
Her black cotton-gloved hands were clasped tightly down in
front of her. And she gazed motionless and gaunt-eyed at the
coffin resting on two chairs across from her, in which all her
hopes and dreams were shut forever. No tears fell from her eyes,
nor did any sound of grief or pain come through her bloodless
and ash-dry lips.

And the grieving song of the mourners gathered there
went softly out across the spring-blossomed campus. Among
the ancient leafing green trees it went and among the great gray
buildings and the red brick ones and across the quiet village,
gently troubling in its vibration the bees and dirt daubers and
butterflies as they sucked and played at the tender white clover
on the wide commons and lawn.

The drowsy students slumped about in their chairs in the
Memorial Library heard it, yawned and went on trying to con-
centrate on their collateral reading. And in the sleepy classrooms
it was the same—if PR equals SW what is the value of V?— If
economics is a science what are the categories for the filling and
satisfying of human desires?— What do the Gestalt psycholo-
gists mean when they say that phenomena are more than the

sum of their parts?— Wherein does the baroque differ from the classical, whether in art or literature?

And some of the stray professors and students passing along Franklin Street stopped, listened a moment, and continued their easy discursive walk toward the post office. And other citizens, stopping a moment in springtime sociability over the impending bond issue for paving this same street, grew silent, took in the protruding fact of a funeral in the distance and resumed their pro and con. A Negro funeral in the cemetery there was a common thing and had been for a hundred and fifty years. And good Negro singing was common too, as well as preaching.

And down in Professor Rochambeau DeRossett's garden an old Negro plowman too stopped his mule Reuben and listened to the mighty funeral hymn of the Negroes blown along on the gentle southwest wind. He stood with grave and high-nostriled blackamoor face, his eyes thoughtful, in which little sparks of musical delight began to show. He had wanted to attend that funeral and help with the singing. He knew they'd have good singing and good preaching at it. And besides, he had known the dead young man and his mother's high hopes for him. But 'Fessor DeRossett said be here and fix his garden, for already it was time that early sass was ready to be cut. He'd been away out west on a mountain where they had a 'scope thing to look through and measure the stars, and was late in getting back to his vegetable planting. Well, anyhow, when a 'fessor said do a thing, a man better do it, for no telling when a fellow might need a friend, a good white friend in the hour of trouble, when trouble comes, as it said in the song. And nobody could be better than a 'fessor from the University. For such 'fessors, as everybody knew, were the most powerful men of all from far and roundabout.

"Giddup, giddup," the old man urged his mule Reuben, his voice softened down in respect to the grief and woe yonder in the distance. "Giddup, giddup," he said again, jerking and jiggling the line the while. And finally like breathing, Reuben leaned his ancient raw bony body, poor as quilting frames, against the collar, and the rickety Boy Dixie plow crinkled the shallow-swelling ground. Then pyang—and the loose-hung plowpoint struck a buried rock and broke clean off. The old plowman chet-chetted with his lips and gave out a few dad-dang-its over his usual bad luck. Still, no help for it, and he would plow no more today. A fact was a fact, and an accident was an accident. 'Fessor couldn't blame him for leaving. And tomorrow would be another day. So he turned Reuben's head into Miz DeRossett's flaming pirus-japonica hedge and hurried off in long strides toward the graveyard, his tall African kingly form moving levelly along. He began humming with his power-ful bass as he went, joining tunefully in with the funeral singing. He sang his dominant, dropping down easily to low C good and strong—

> *"The earth in dust and ashes hid*
> *Before the awful sign,*
> *The moon ran down in purple stream*
> *The sun forebore to shine—*
> *Then grieve, grieve, grieve,*
> *For death's a hard trial."*

He went on by the old Episcopal church, ivy-wrapped and haunted by chattering sparrows, singing as he went—

> *"The bells of death ring in the night*
> *To wake men to their doom,*
> *Bright sparkles in the churchyard shine*
> *To light them to their tomb—*
> *Then grieve, grieve, grieve,*
> *For death's a hard trial—"*

And in Graham Hall, Professor Allison Haywood was holding his class, Pedagogy 73, the same being The Curriculum, Its Principles and Practices. "One of the basic difficulties in building a proper curriculum for the teacher," he was saying, "arises from the fact that there seems to be a difference between subjects of study which are culturally broadening and those which are practical in their benefit. There seems to be a battle going on between, for example, the humanities in university life and the vocational and technical disciplines. As, well you might say, a devotee of both, I feel the dilemma in a rather personal way. Excuse me a moment." He rose, moved across the room, and raised the window higher. He stood a moment listening to the music coming from the cemetery. The students watched him and smiled. They knew his weakness. He was caught in the pull of the singing and his avocation as student of Negro and folk mores. "I've decided to let you young gentlemen go somewhat early today," he said a little shamefacedly.

And with that he gathered up his papers and hurried from the room. The young men clattered down the stairs like a gang of heavy-footed goats, but Professor Haywood had already got his hat and notebook and was ahead of them on his way to the graveyard.

And in the cemetery the thin, toilworn mother stood as before, her eyes dry as whip sockets. The singing had stopped now and the old Negro preacher, pastor of the church where the boy and mother were members, was reading gently and con-solingly from the open Bible in his hand. "Blessed are they that mourn," he read, "for they shall be comforted. Blessed are the meek, for they shall inherit the earth." The gentle words broke sweetly in the soft still air. "Let your light so shine before men that they may see your good works and glorify your father which is in heaven."

The mother had heard the Sermon on the Mount many a time before. But the words now read again and here on the occasion of her great tragedy brought her a vague but authorita-tive comfort. They had an even more holy sound here in the midst of her grief than ever they had before. It was almost as if a kindly and familiar hand had touched her or even a sheltering and protecting arm had reached around her. The tight black-gloved hands began to relax, and presently she pushed her wadded handkerchief against her mouth and closed her eyes. The melt of moisture was beginning to form beneath her lashes.

The old preacher closed his Bible and spoke gently. "Our young brother was cut off in the full promise of his prime," he said. "The cold wind of death has nipped the bud of his young days. And even as it is writ, he that goes down to the grave shall come up no more and thou shalt seek me in the morning but I shall not be. But even say so, I know that my Redeemer liveth and that I shall stand at the latter day upon the earth. And though after my skin, worms destroy my body to pieces, yet in my flesh shall I see God. Let us pray."

All but the mother bowed their heads. Her eyes were still closed. "Our Heavenly Father," he prayed, "we know that we are nothing. As a flower soon cut down or as a wind what comes and is gone and known no more, we are nothing. Thou art all. Thy ways are mysterious and past our feeble understanding and we can only trust and believe in thee. And oh, Father, teach us faith. Teach us to be humble and accept the good and the bad alike, the dark days and the bright days, the sunshine and the rain. For as we love thee, thou certainly lovest us. And in thy love thou canst do us no evil. And I most specifically pray thy comfort on this grieving mother. Let her see that all is for a purpose. And that her boy was needed in Paradise else thou wouldst not have sent for him. Teach us patience, acceptance of thy will. Even as she has lost a son, yea the more surely she shall find her eternal father. We ask it all in the name of our sweet Lord and Saviour, Jesus Christ. Amen."

"Amen," said the mourners.

And then the coffin was let swiftly down into the grave, the boards were crossed over it, and the digging shovels began to pile the dirt rapidly in.

"Ashes to ashes and dust to dust," intoned the preacher as the first thr-r-ump sounded.

The old plowman led forth in a hymn now, and the people joined richly and sonorously in. The shovels kept vying with one another as the song went on.

> "Well King Jesus said, said 'Gimme some rest,
> Some rest from earthly trile,'
> And the words come back from the father's throne—
> 'A little while, in a little while.'
> Then blow the trumpet and shout the praise,
> And ring the bells of heaven roun'—

> *Old death gonna be my folding bed,*
> *Lie down, lie down!"*

The mother opened her eyes. The grave was filled and being roached up now by the patting shovels. The pine head-board and footboard were put in place. A few of the neighbors came forward with handfuls of redbud sprays, golden bell, and winter jessamine and a few broken branches of sweet breath of spring which they laid on the mound. The mother saw Professor Haywood behind the group around the grave. He had arrived just before the song began. Her boy would have been pleased to know that the great Dr. Haywood had come in honor of his funeral. He had read one of Dr. Haywood's books he'd bor-rowed from a Negro teacher and thought it was wonderful. It told all about what the Negro in the South must do to raise himself. The water in her eyes formed a little faster. She wiped it away with her handkerchief. The song went on, and then as some of the group shifted about she saw Dr. Haywood more plainly. He was standing with one foot on a low tombstone and had a small notebook half-hidden in his hand, and he was writing in it. She knew he was copying down the words of the song. He was always like that, collecting knowledge—learning, learning.

The song ended, the funeral was over, and the neighbors began to drift away. Most of them had jobs around in the community as cooks, yardmen, or cleaners by the odd hour, and they had to get back to their work.

Dr. Haywood slid his notebook into his pocket and came toward the mother. He had his hat off now in respect to her and the occasion.

"I'm sorry—sorry to see this, Katie," he said. She nodded. "It was, it was—" he went on a little haltingly.

"He was nineteen. We called him Bobo," she said.

"Bobo!" he said shocked. "I hadn't heard of it, Katie."

"He was a good worker," she said.

"Yes, a good worker," murmured Professor Haywood. He turned and looked heavily at the flower-spread grave. "Last winter he raked the leaves out of my yard."

"He ketched his death up there at Davis Hall a week ago—that cold day, suh," she went on tonelessly. "He was washing the windows and a chill struck him."

"Bad, too bad," said Professor Haywood grievingly. Then his voice rose irritated, a touch of anger in it. "Why didn't he take better care of himself. He should have! Yes. Why didn't he!"

"Yessuh, Professor," Katie said, "but he was working to save up his money, suh." Her gaunt tearless eyes looked over at Dr. Haywood. "He was planning to go up north this fall," she added, "where he could start to college."

Dr. Haywood was silent a moment. He stared at the ground, then turned aside and put on his hat. But he didn't go away. He stood there. Presently he said, "I hope you'll let me know if I can help you in any way, Katie—I'll speak to Mrs. Haywood. Perhaps she'd have some extra work for you—or something. I'll speak to her."

"Thank you, sir," she said.

A moment more Professor Haywood stood there. Then he went off across the cemetery, his steps quickening as he walked. He touched the notebook in his pocket. The new song he'd copied was a real find. It would just fit into chapter five of his new book on the Cultural Backgrounds of the Southern Negro. But strangely the fact brought him no elation. He mounted the front steps of Graham Hall, then looked back toward the cemetery. The place was deserted now except for the dark straight figure of the mother who still stood by the grave in wordless communion with her perished son. He went on into the building. The bell was already ringing for the next class.

Fare Thee Well

~~~~~~

I *t was an early summer morning* and a little mulatto boy of six or seven was sitting on a box in a rough bare tenant farmhouse room there in the wide Carolina fields. A young woman, nicely dressed and pretty, with rather tawny dark skin was packing a trunk. Her eyes were red from weeping. After a while the boy looked up and asked, "How long 'fore we're ready, Mammy?"

"Purty soon now," she answered. Her voice was husky and tight. "In a hurry to go?"

"No'm," he replied soberly after a moment. He twisted about on the box, knocking his heels together in ill ease, and the woman went on packing. She took three or four photographs from the floor and put them into the trunk.

"Thought you said leave 'em, Mammy."

"I'll take 'em now," she murmured in a low voice.

The boy bent over and stared at one of the photographs. "Why you wanter take him?"

"Why not, sonny!"

"I don't like him." And he kept on kicking his heels.

"Think of all the candy he's brought you."

"I don't like him." She made no reply, and soon the boy went on with his querying. "How far us going, Mammy?"

"A long ways, sonny."

"On the old train?"

"And on a steamboat and purty water."

"And will there be plenty of bicycles and elevunts where we're going like you said?"

"Elephants, buster."

"Elevunts, Mammy."

"We'll see heaps of things," she said.

The boy took two large glass marbles from his pocket, got down on the floor and began to shoot one at the other. Presently he stopped and sat on his haunches thinking.

"Can I run and see Uzzy 'fore us go?"

"You won't have time."

"Wuh gonna drive his little goat and cyart—"

"Cart."

"—Cart—this evening." He went up to his mother and leaned his head against her. "Us got a new bow and wire key for the yoke." He suddenly flung himself against her, weeping. "I don't wanter leave Uzzy."

She looked down at him and stroked his face. "Maybe you'll have a new bicycle when we get there. It will go faster than the little goat."

The boy grew quiet. "With a tool bag?" he asked.

"And a new pump in it."

"And clincher tires maybe?"

"Yes, and bright spokes and—and bright spokes."

"And I can ride back sometime and see Uzzy, Mammy?"

"Yes, when you grow great big. Go play with your marbles while I shut the trunk." She closed the trunk and buckled down the straps. "Look out and see if Sandy's coming."

The boy looked out and called, "Can't see him nowhere. There's my bantling rooster by the stable." And then he whimpered, "I don't wanter leave Charlie Boy."

"Leave him for Uzzy."

"Wanter take him wiv me."

"The conductor man won't let him ride on the train, sonny."

"Will he let me ride?"

"You can ride. And you can listen to the train blow too."

"And hear it choo-chooing," he called jubilantly.

"And see the smoke from the engine."

"Will they be coal cyars—cars and freight cars, Mammy?"

"And passenger cars and flatcars and all kinds of cars."

"Painted red?"

"Painted red and all kinds of colors—yellow and brown, and some of them black."

The boy gazed thoughtfully out of the window. In a moment he turned and stared at his mother. "And will the train go fast like Mr. Ed's car?"

"Oh—yes—oh, faster, faster. The trees will go by zip-zup."

He turned and gazed again through the window.

"Yonder do come somebody," he said, "maybe it's Sandy for the trunk. It's Mr. Ed, Mammy."

"Go out in the yard and play with your marbles, sonny."

"I don't like him, Mammy." He came up to her again and caught hold of her dress. "He's gonna hurt you."

"Good gracious, silly. He won't hurt Mother."

"Yes'm he might."

He put his hand timidly on her shoulder. "How come last night when he was here he make you cry so? And now you're crying again." She dabbed her eyes with her handkerchief.

"Now you see Mother's not crying. Run along."

"I like Sandy, Mammy."

"Yes, sonny."

"You don't like Sandy."

"Oh, yes I do."

"I mean love him."

"Run along."

"He loves you, Mammy."

"Sonny!"

"He told me so—he did. I want him for my favver. Please, Mammy."

"Run along I tell you."

Outside a car stopped before the house. The boy went out and a man's voice was heard speaking to him.

"Hello, buster," the man said.

"Mammy's been crying again," the boy's hard little voice replied.

Soon the man came into the room. He was a well-to-do young white farmer of thirty-five or more. He stood looking at the woman sitting on the trunk. She got up and stood straight and tall before him. For a moment she stood so without speaking. And then she spoke.

"Goodby, Mr. Ed—Ed."

"I come by to drive you to the station." He reached out his hand and hers came out spontaneously to meet it. "The boy can ride in the pickup with Sandy," he added, still holding her hand in his.

"And all the neighbors out looking, Mr. Ed?"

"Well—don't—well, I don't mind now," he interposed hastily. "I never knew till today what it meant for you to go."

"I didn't either," she whispered softly.

Outside the bantam rooster was heard squawking, and the boy rushed in with him in his arms.

"I caught him, Mammy. Won't they let him ride on the train, Mr. Ed?"

"Sure, and we'll get a little box in town to put him in."

The boy eyed them. "Why you holding Mammy's hand so?"

"I'm telling Mr. Ed goodby," the woman laughed, pulling her hand away. "Go to the kitchen and get that sack from the nail and put him in it."

"And cut a small hole so he can get air," Mr. Ed added.

The boy talked to the rooster as he went out. "You gonna ride on the train, Charlie Boy, and look froo the windows."

When he was gone the man turned toward the woman, "I reckon you despise me, Lalie."

"No, I don't," and she looked at him directly.

"Lord, you're sweet and beautiful."

"But she's a lot sweeter," she spoke up almost sharply.

The man stood for a long time looking at the floor. After a while he said with sudden and boyish forlornness, "She'll never fill your place."

"Still, you're marrying her."

"But that don't mean you have to leave."

"It does too. My place is filled."

"But why'n the name of heaven leave and have to face the world by yourself? Lalie, you won't have anybody to look after you."

"I'm not afraid of it. I can sew, wash—find something to do there in Chicago."

"Well, so you do despise me."

"No."

The man cried out vehemently, "Ain't it natural for a man to want a family and take his right place in the neighborhood and be something?"

"Yes, natural for him to want children, his kind of children. So goodby."

"Well, it can't be any other way."

"It can't. And I'm going where my boy'll have no remembrance of all this disgrace. Someday he'll come back a man—be somebody maybe."

"Still got your dreaming," he muttered narrowly.

The pickup truck was heard driving up outside. The man suddenly burst out, "If I could stand up before the world and tell them what you are and what you mean to me, then I'd feel right. But it can't be, it never can be."

"No, it never can be," she whispered.

After a moment he said, "Well, I'll go." He smiled at her funnily. "That's the way these things are, you know."

"What things?" she said suddenly and again almost sharply. "And as she says in that book you gave me, 'Fare thee well and fare thee well.'" He looked at her, his face thoughtful.

The boy came in with the rooster's head stuck through a hole in the sack.

"Tell your father goodby, sonny."

"He ain't my favver."

The man tried to take the boy in his arms. "Goodby, buster."

The boy flew to his mother sobbing. "He ain't my favver. I don't like him."

"Oh God, you're crazy, Lalie!" the man cried and turned abruptly and went out.

Sandy came up on the porch outside and called, "Is the trunk in there?"

The woman sat rocking back and forth with the boy in her arms.

"Lalie, is the trunk in there?" Sandy called again.

"Yes—yes, Sandy, it's in here," she answered. "And we're all ready." And Sandy, honest and black, came resolutely in and took up the trunk. His lips were tight, and he said nothing.

Land of Nod

The two of us were thinning the long spraddle-legged cotton stalks for the siding plow to follow—all in the sweet June weather. I was in the lead naturally, me being me and "always in such a swivet," as Uncle Arthur said, and Uncle Arthur was behind, he being who he was and "always taking it easy and looking out after his weak back," as I said. I was fifteen and stout and strong-minded for my age and was helping clean out the cotton because of sympathy for my Aunt Lillian. She had in her late thirties, some few years before, married Uncle Arthur in his bachelor middle age to reform him, and as everybody knew was having a poverty-stricken time of her life.

That morning too my father had said, "Go down there and help your Uncle Arth with his cotton. The grass is about to take it. No, go help your Aunt Lillian, I mean."

Yes, Uncle Arth was a poor provider, in fact hardly any provider at all. He instinctively shied away from anything that meant sweat and hard work. And already I, who belonged to a hard-working self-reliant family, had pretty much lost all respect for him.

Aunt Lillian had reformed her husband all right. Since the day of their marriage three years before, Uncle Arth had not touched a drop of liquor. A wonderful moral reform it was. But he who had at least a little bit of get-up-and-get in his drinking days now had lost even that since he quit liquor. It was as if he felt so proud of his new-found character that his self-esteem and self-satisfaction were sufficient to sustain his inner man in his laziness. He felt no prickings of conscience as his wife ironed and washed and milked the scrawny ticky cow and did what she could in selling a bit of butter and a few eggs now and then to make ends meet and to tithe something for foreign missionary work, which subject of the heathen lay heavy in her tender heart. Hadn't he quit drinking, and what more could you ask!

Maybe in his slubbery way Uncle Arth loved Aunt Lillian. Maybe he didn't. I didn't know. But I knew he loved the courthouse all right. Nothing suited him better than to hang around the loafers over there and mix among the political deadbeats and perennial buzzard candidates for office every chance he got.

Finally, somehow he had got up brass and energy enough to meet with the right precinct boss and so was appointed a rural justice of the peace. And sweet it was to his ears when the first defendant addressed him as "Jedge." A feeble-witted Negro boy named Jay Gould McLean it was who had robbed one of Aunt Lillian's hens' nests and who Uncle Arthur, much to my disgust —for I was there at the time—and Aunt Lillian's patient protestation, declared must be tried. And spitting a slew of tobacco juice and eyeing a pocket of space in the northeast part of the horizon where perhaps he saw some image of majesty that resided there as he deliberated, the judge pronounced a fine of fifty cents on Jay Gould and ordered him to work it out then and there picking cotton for him, the said judge. "The power of the law must be upheld," he said. And all that day Uncle Arth had sat about overseeing Jay Gould as he worked out his fine.

Since early morning now Uncle Arth and I had been at the chopping, and it was getting on toward ten o'clock and the air was becoming a little steamy. Every now and then he stopped, looked biliously around the world, cocked his eye toward the northeast—a funny habit he had—wiped his forehead with his sleeve and with his middle finger carefully pushed back the looping strands of his tobacco-drenched moustache. Then he lazily resumed his chopping, making one laggard stroke while I made two or three. I heard him muttering to himself there behind me.

"What say?" I said.

"I say you're always working like your britches was full of red ants," he growled.

Without looking around, I spoke right back—"I reckon it's better'n having the dead lice dropping off you."

Oh yes, I was brash and spoke full out at him because I had so little respect for Uncle Arthur and because, as my folks said, I myself had such a high temper.

"Uhm, uhm, listen at him," Uncle Arthur mumbled, and he stood a moment, leaning his chin on the knob-end of his hoe-handle and staring longingly down toward the cool creek forest half a mile away. "Whew, it's gonna be a scorcher!" he called.

"Come on, Uncle Arth, you've not even started sweating yet!" I called back. "Cool, man, it's cool compared to what it's gonna be along about two o'clock. Remember—when the fall comes you want a bale or two of cotton to sell, want to feel that good old money jingling in your pockets."

"You and your money!" he cackled.

"Aunt Lillian's money then," I answered testily. "And besides, the almanac prophesies it's likely to be wet weather later this month and we want to get this cotton cleaned up and plowed and ready for it."

Uncle Arth swore by the almanac, but I didn't. Already from my reading in my school books I didn't.

"You and your prophecy!" Uncle Arthur said.

"I know this is sorry work for a judge," I half-jeered, "but the Bible do say a man's got to live by the sweat of his brow."

"You and your—" Then he stopped for, like all the people round and about in the Little Bethel neighborhood, he didn't dare speak disrespectfully of the Holy Book. He resumed his pecking sickly strokes, and soon I was out to the end of my row and coming back on another toward him.

Later a mule and buggy came along the lane beyond the rail fence nearby, driven by a Negro youth all dressed out in a blue suit and panama hat and stiff collar with a yellow tie, and with a white rose stuck in the lapel of his coat. By his side sat a babyish Negro girl in a white muslin frock and blue scarf and with a great droopy yellow beribboned hat hanging sideways on her head. Uncle Arth heard the buggy wheels and hoof thuds and looked off as the vehicle stopped beyond the fence. The youth pulled off his hat and held it extended in front of him, then called across the fence toward us as he bowed his body respectfully forward.

"Mawning, suh," he said.

"Yeah?" Uncle Arth grunted queryingly, eyeing him.

"Is you the jedge, suh?" the Negro inquired.

I spat disgustedly as I saw the judicial feeling begin taking hold of Uncle Arth.

"I am that," he said loftily and sternly. And he stamped his hoe against the ground and stood with it straight beside him like a Roman soldier with a spear. "And I reckon I can guess what you want."

The girl slapped her little hands together, leaned over sideways and burst into a cascade of high giggles, then as if abashed, bowed her droopy hat over and sat silent. But I could see her chubby small shoulders shaking with stuffed-in merriment.

"Well, yes, suh, us wants to git j'ined—married, suh," said the youth.

"You do, eh?" said Uncle Arth, still standing straight and stern and not moving.

"Yes, suh."

"And what does the girl say?"

The girl threw up her hands again and let out a little shrill hilarious scream and rocked from side to side.

"Well, I can see she's as big a fool as you are," Uncle Arth called out. "How old are you?"

"'Bout eighteen, suh," said the Negro.

"And the yaller gal—how old is she?"

"How old's you?" I heard the young man murmur.

"I's 'bout sixteen," said the girl in a small but remarkably clear childlike voice.

"All right then," Uncle Arth called in this commanding manner. "Take hands."

The youth put his panama hat back on his head, took one of the girl's hands in his and held it up before him. And Uncle Arth intoned loudly through the warm spring air—

"Nought's a nought,
Figger's a figger,
Kiss your bride,
You dirty nigger!"

The boy and the girl sat still. The fields were still, and I stood still in them. Only the creaking of the harness hames was heard as the mule's great gullet head dropped down and the huge whiskered lips began gnawing hungrily at the sparse grass in the fence jamb. The youth looked out sideways and finally said, "Is they any more, Jedge?"

"Ain't no more," Uncle Arth said.

"You mean that's all Jedge?"

"All," said Uncle Arth loudly, "and it'll hold you till the cows come home."

"Then we's married, Jedge?" the bridegroom timidly called.

"Yes, you're married," said Uncle Arth roughly. "I pronounce you man and wife. And it'll cost you a dollar." He held out his hand before him and then shouted, "Do as I say—kiss your bride."

The young husband gave the girl a tiny bump with his mouth against her cheek, at which her body swayed and undulated like a cornstalk in a wind. And there was no giggle from her now.

The Negro got out of the buggy, climbed over the fence, and came up to Uncle Arth bareheaded and with his vast respect. He put a silver dollar in the judge's still-outstretched hand, and the "court" dropped it carelessly into his shirt pocket as if it were of no importance to him at all now. The bridegroom began bowing and backing away.

"Thankee, suh, thankee, suh."

"You're mashing down my young cotton!" Uncle Arth suddenly yelled, and he lifted his hoe threateningly. The youth slammed his hat on, turned, and vaulted over the fence light as a deer. He sprang into the buggy, and he and his bride drove on down the road, sitting straight and stiff side by side. Only once did they look back—a quick little snatched glance. Uncle Arth rested on his upright hoe-handle again and gazed after them, his moustache wiggling in a sardonic smile. I looked at him in swelling anger.

"Seems like you might have asked them their names," I finally said with all the sarcasm my young years could command.

"It don't make no difference," said Uncle Arth. "And look," he continued, gesturing off, "she's got her head laying over on his shoulder now. First huckleberry thicket they find they'll stop and go to it."

"That was a lowdown thing to do!" I said fiercely.

"Do how?" he queried with a chuckle, as he swiftly took the dollar from his shirt pocket, and stowed it deep inside his old trousers.

"To pretend to marry them like that. To say that mean piece of poetry over them like that—to—to—" I was stuttering with rage.

"It don't make no difference. I learned that when I was a boy."

"Learned what?"

"Learned it don't make no difference—not with niggers."

"They're not even married, and their children will—"

"Of course they're married. You heard me pronounce them man and wife."

"Ah, Lord! What a way to treat a human being!"

"A nigger ain't a human being."

"And where do you get that idea?" I snorted, and I began hoeing my row furiously again.

Uncle Arthur smiled and walked along with me, his hoe in his hand. I could feel his self-satisfied judgmenting look.

"From the best place in the world to get ideas. You ought to know—being as you're so smart in scripture and have read the Bible through near 'bout twice, your proud Mammy says."

"Well, the Bible don't say a Negro's not a human being, it never says that!"

"Oh, yes it does, says so when you put two and two together. Long ago my daddy pointed it all out to me—and his daddy before him. And I've hearn Preacher Wicker say the same." And now cocking his head to one side, he put on his legal manner again, interrogating me, as if I were a defendant hauled before him. "How many children did Adam and Eve have?"

I humored him. "Well, they had Cain and Abel and—"

"Stop right there. Cain and Abel's enough. Now Cain and Abel got into a fight, didn't they?"

"It was Cain's fight. He picked up a rock and slew his brother." And I chopped faster. Uncle Arthur followed along.

"So he did, and I believe it. Then what happened to Cain?"

"God put a curse on him, a mark on him, and he fled."

"And where did he go?"

"The Bible says he went up into the land of Nod."

"Ah-hah, that's just what he did. Then what happened?"

"So you're coming to that business of his finding his wife up there. Yes, I see what you're after!"

"That's just what I am," he spoke up triumphantly. And then his face deepened with the hypocritical pious look I knew so well from the communion Sundays in Little Bethel Church when he officiated around the white tablecloth with the wine cup and the bits of damp clammy bread. And now he went on sanctimoniously. "And I want you to know that no matter what some these here smart folks say—which your Mammy says you read after—I believe the Bible from led to led."

"Oh, yes, you say you do." I was boiling.

"Yes, I do. And the Bible do say in Genesis four, verses fifteen, sixteen, and seventeen, that God set a mark on Cain and Cain went up into the land of Nod—"

"'And Cain went out from the presence of the Lord, and dwelt in the land of Nod, on the east of Eden,'" I corrected sharply.

"Ahm, yes, that's right. And then what do it say?"

"'And Cain knew his wife; and she conceived, and bore Enoch: and he builded a city—'"

"Whoa, that's enough! Now who was Cain's wife? They wasn't but one woman on earth at that time, was they—Eve, his own mother? No sir, no other woman. Well, I'll tell you what's the truth—Cain cohabited up with one of these here female gorillas—you've seen 'em in the circus at Raleigh, seen what flat noses and big lips they've got just like a nigger—"

"Aw, go to the—go to—" I sputtered. And I hoed even more furiously. Uncle Arthur still walked along by me.

"And that's the pime-blank truth," he went on. "Cain's children were animals. And they were niggers. And niggers are animals, and they ain't got no souls. They were born of an animal, a gorilla. That's how the nigger race got started. And being the children of a gorilla, as I say, they ain't got no soul.

You may not believe it, but most of the folks in this neighborhood believe it."

"Yes, they sure do," I sneered. "They use it for an excuse to oppress and keep the Negro people down. And the big politicians in Raleigh believe it and use it for the same reason. I see it from reading *The News and Observer* and from friends—from friends I have known." My lips were trembling and I was about ready to burst into angry tears. I flung down my hoe. "And as for your old cotton I wouldn't chop another hill of it if it wasn't for poor Aunt Lillian that you browbeat and use like a doormat to wipe your feet on—the way Papa says."

Turning, I went ragingly down across the little field to the spring branch to get myself some water.

"Lordy mercy, he's madder'n a wet hen," Uncle Arth shrilled after me. I made no answer. And sitting by the spring, I fashioned a little cup of some green red oak leaves and drank my belly full of the sweet clear water.

Presently looking across the fields I saw Uncle Arth on his way to his shack of a house there. I knew where he was headed now—over to town to visit the courthouse gang and spend his dollar. And sure enough, in a few minutes I saw him drive his little horse hitched up to a roadcart, from around behind the shack. Aunt Lillian came out on the corner-sagging decrepit porch and spoke to him. "Will you be back for supper, Arthur?" I heard her call in her meek way. And I also heard her husband's gruff reply that he had legal business in town that might keep him late and for her to go ahead and eat by herself.

And so he drove happily away. I knew what legal business it was—sitting around the courthouse and chewing the rag and eating peanuts and bananas and cocoanut candy till his dollar was gone, and listening to the deadbeats talk too and argue about the corruption of the Republican party, and then after that all about the heathen practices of the lost souls in India and China who had never heard of Jesus Christ and Him crucified and so were doomed to eternal punishment—babies, young people, and old people.

I got up stiffly and went on back to my work. And there across the rows, with her house duties done now, came Aunt

Lillian to take her beloved husband's hoe and labor in his stead. I muttered fiercely to myself, "Ehm—ehm, aih Lord!"

And so whish—whish—whish—went our hoes again in the soft loamy earth as the morning wore on. And the moist feel of the month of June was in the air around us.

"It's a mighty purty day, ain't it?" Aunt Lillian said. "You can smell the sweet bay blooms down in the swamp."

I was so swelled up with bitterness that I made no answer. And we chopped on.

Soon Aunt Lillian's clear voice rose in one of her beloved hymns, and soon too her strong chopping strokes fell into the rhythm of the piece. I was a sucker for music. And in spite of myself I was before long joining in with her. Out across the burning fields our singing went—

> *"Can we whose souls are lighted*
> *By wisdom from on high,*
> *Can we to men benighted*
> *The lamp of life deny?"*

I made my boyish alto harmonize now with her fresh soprano, and somewhat satirically so, though kind heart that she was she would never notice it.

> *"Salvation! O Salvation!*
> *The joyful sound proclaim,*
> *Till earth's remotest nation*
> *Has learned Messiah's name!"*

And now I called out loudly, "Next verse! Let's make it ring, Aunt Lillian. Make it ring!"

She gave me a grateful happy smile—and we did, all about the heathen ones lost in darkness far away—

> *"In vain with lavish kindness*
> *The gifts of God are strown,*
> *The heathen in his blindness*
> *Bows down to wood and stone—*
> *Bows down to wood and stone."*

Lay My Body Down

Tilsy McNeill, a thin hollow-eyed Negro woman, thirty years old, was ironing clothes in her cabin one hot May afternoon. Several garments she had just ironed were hanging over a rocker before the fireplace, and a pile of rough-dry clothes were on the bed at the left. She hurried to and fro, trying to finish quickly the task before her, but more than once she stopped her flying steps and twisted her head and shoulders as if to ease a dull pain gnawing at the back of her neck. Suddenly with the weight of her pressure upon the ironing board, the rocking chair toppled over, and clothes and all fell to the floor. She clutched at the iron and then drew her hand away with a cry of pain. Setting the iron to the fire, she ran to a pan of water on the table and soused her hand in it and stood shuddering and wiping her streaming hot face with her apron. Charlie, her little black barefoot boy of ten, came into the cabin, carrying a hoe in his hand.

"Mommee," he said, "Mr. Johnson—" He stopped abruptly, seeing his mother with her hand to her face. "What's the matter? Your toofache worse?"

Tilsy whirled at him. "Look at you dragging a hoe in this house and bad luck with it!" she yelled. "Get it out of here, boy, get it out!" He threw the hoe out through the door behind him. "Bring me that soda box in the kitchen," she groaned. "Quick, I tell you! I done burnt my hand to the bone." Charlie ran into the kitchen and reappeared with the soda. Tilsy dried her hand, spread the soda on it, and wrapped it up in a rag which she got from the bureau drawer, talking at him as she did so. "Why you coming to the house this time of day, and the sun two hours high? You go out there and gather up that hoe and get right back to the cotton patch. Fade from here or I'll tan your hide with a stick!"

"Mr. Johnson run us out'n the cotton field," Charlie said timidly.

"He did?" Tilsy exclaimed, starting angrily towards him, "And you a-slubbering your work, that's why! I told you, I told you and Sina to chop your rows clean."

"Mommee," said Charlie, backing away from her storm of wrath, "he said you'd oughta keep with us when we chops. That's what the man said."

"He did! Well, how in the name of God do he 'spect me to get Mis' Johnson's washing and ironing done if I have to stay in the fields too?" She hurried back to her ironing. "Did he pay you for what you chopped?"

"No'm," Charlie answered, "he just got a switch and driv us off."

"Treating you like that!" Tilsy stormed in the air. She raised the iron in her hand, "I wish to Jesus I could scrush his head in with this here iron, I do! Where's Sina?" And she fell feverishly back to work.

"She's coming along behind with Babe," said Charlie as he edged softly toward the bureau.

Tilsy hung a shirt on the chair and went on ironing another. Charlie watched her as he stealthily opened the bureau drawer.

"You step to the woodpile and get me a bucket of chips," Tilsy said. She caught sight of his hand in the drawer. "Hear me? What you doing?"

"Nothing," came Charlie's small answer.

"Yeh, you are," Tilsy insisted. "I know, you're after them there fishing hooks I hid."

"I just wanted to look at 'em a speck, please'm."

"A speck! Let you get your fingers on 'em, and in a jook of a sheep's tail you'd be in the creek fishing." Her voice rose stern and threatening in the sweaty air. "Fetch them chips and lemme hear no more about it."

She made a motion toward him with the iron, and he backed out through the door. She began folding up the dry-ironed clothes and putting them into a bag, and now and then she twisted her head and sucked her teeth in pain. Charlie came back with the chips and dumped them on the fire. He sidled over toward her and plucked at her apron. "Mommee," he coaxed pleadingly. "I could catch us some yellow bellies if you'd lemme go to the creek."

Tilsy turned on him wrathfully. "Listen to me! You ain't going down to no creek and drownd yourself, you hear? I want you to take this bag of clothes and run 'cross the road to Mis' Johnson's and tell her I'll have the others done sometime tonight."

"I—I don't want to go over there," he stammered in an all-of-a-sudden fright. "Mr. Johnson cussed at me while ago, I tell you."

"Can't help it," his mother said, shaking her head. "We got to have some grub to last over Sunday. And tell her to pay you for that cotton chopping," she continued. "They promised you a quarter apiece. And with fifty cents you could go over to Buie's Creek and get some Baltimore meat at Mr. Haire's store."

A loud squealing suddenly set up in the kitchen. "Lordy," she moaned, "sump'n's happened to Babe. Run see what's the matter."

Charlie started out at the rear, but the door opened, and Babe, a little chocolate-colored creature of three or four years, yelling loudly, pushed her way in. Sina, black and about nine, with bare legs as thin as sticks, and wearing a slip of a dirty dress, followed her.

"What ails that baby, Sina?" Tilsy demanded grimly.

"She—she hurt her nose," Sina piped timidly.

Tilsy picked up the baby and crooned to it. "Poor thing, you've hurt yourself." She turned darkly to Sina. "Sina McNeill, I done told you about taking care of this child. And I oughta whip you. Now tell me what you done to her." She set Babe down.

"I ain't done nothing, Mommee," Sina protested.

"Ain't done nothing!" Tilsy shrilled. "No, you ain't. First you and Charlie chop your cotton so sorry you get run out'n the field, and we needing every cent we can get our hands on! Then next you come walking in so high and mighty, bringing Babe with her head 'bout busted open."

She picked the child up again and wiped her nose, at the same time putting her hand to her own jaw with a mouth-twist of pain.

"I—I was trying to get her some bread from the cupboard," Sina began explaining hesitantly, "and I couldn't find none. And she kept a-whining and saying there was some in there. Then she fou't me off and climbed up to see for herself, and she fell and hurt her nose."

"The pore thing's hungry again," Tilsy sighed, as Babe began to cry softly against her breast. "There's a piece of bread at the back of the cook table. Bring her that." And she added bitterly, "I don't reckon the flies have worked it to death."

Sina hurried out of the room into the kitchen, returning with the bread. Tilsy set Babe on a chair, where she began eating greedily, and then she hurried back to her work. "Lord help me," she groaned, "I'll never finish this ironing today. And Mis' Johnson's bound to have it for church tomorrow."

"Can't I—can't I help you do sump'n, Mommee?" Sina queried tremulously.

Tilsy looked at her sharply, then turned her head away and ironed in silence. Charlie stood helplessly in the back of the room, looking around and scratching his leg with his toe. Suddenly Tilsy sat down and stuffed her apron to her face, her body heaving with sobs. Sina and Charlie looked miserably at each other.

"Mom, I'm gonna take the clothes over there right now," Charlie said brightly and sturdily.

A sob broke from his mother.

"What make her cry, Charlie?" Sina asked softly.

"I dunno, less'n it's her teeth," he replied wretchedly.

Hearing her mother sob, Babe began to cry again. Sina went up to Tilsy. "Mommee," she said, "you want me to wrap up the iron and put it to your head?" Tilsy reached out convulsively and drew the little girl to her. Tears began to pour from Sina's eyes and her lips crinkled into a cry.

Tilsy raised her tear-wet face. "Come here, Babe, to your

mommee," she said. Babe rushed into her mother's arms, and
Tilsy rocked to and fro, holding her to her bosom. She started
singing, and Babe grew quiet, the other children hovering close
to her—

> *"I walk in the morning, walk in the evening—*
> *O baby, don'a you cry.*
> *Work and pray and work and pray,*
> *With Jesus by and by.*
> *Lemme lay this body down, lemme lay this body down—"*

She bent and kissed Babe, with Sina tearfully clinging to
her.

> *"With trial and trouble, trial and trouble—*
> *O baby, husha your cry—"*

She stopped singing and looked at them now with tear-
washed shining eyes.

"Mommee, can't I help you none?" Charlie gulped, his
little black paw clutching at her shoulder.

Sina wiped her eyes with the hem of her mother's dress
and asked, "You want me to iron and let you rest now?"

"That's all right," Tilsy said, "—that's all right. Sometimes
I forget how much I love you. And you're good to me—good.
And don't feel bad 'bout me talking rough to you. My head's
been just about to kill me, and I got so tired—I—I—" She put
Babe down and stood up. "Now run on and forget I've been
mean to you. We'll make it somehow," she smiled. "Things can't
go against us forever. We gonna make it somehow."

"I'll take the clothes now, Mom," Charlie chirped, "if you
wants me to."

"All right, honey," she answered, now back at the ironing.
"And if Mis' Johnson ain't got the money handy, ask her to let
you have a little side meat for the chopping. And tell her I'll fetch
all the wash about dark."

"All right'm," said Charlie. And picking up the clothes
bag, he hurried away with it.

"And Sina, you get the gallon bucket and hurry over to Mr. Green's and ask him to let us have enough meal for tonight and tomorrow," Tilsy went on. "I owe him for a peck already, but I know he'll trust us again. Tell him I'll pay him back next week somehow." Sina got the bucket. "And take Babe along with you and pick some flowers if you find any. Them in the vase is done dead."

Sina lingered a moment. "Mommee," she said, "you won't cry no more, will you? Me'n Charlie'll get some money to help you yet. We're gonna work hard—"

"You're smart as a bee, honey," and Tilsy kissed her on the forehead. "And what I'd do without you to stick by me I don't know. Go ahead now and get back purty quick."

"Yes'm," said Sina, taking Babe by the hand. "Come on, Babe," she said, "we're gonna get some flowers and see the birdies hopping by," and they went out through the door.

Tilsy bowed her head as she worked and breathed a prayer, "Lord, Lord, stay with me and my children." She ironed away in silence, now and then sucking her teeth. Presently Charlie burst into the room with a scamper of feet. He was panting and his eyes were wide with fright.

"Mommee! Mom!" he squealed, as he ran up to her and buried his face in her apron.

"What's all the ruckus about? You look like you seen Old Scratch!" she cried. "What is it?"

"Mommee, Mommee, Pap's out there in the road," he gulped.

"Your pap?" queried Tilsy in a scared voice.

"I seen him a-coming and I scatted back to tell you." He looked up at her still holding to her apron. "He'll hurt you. I know he will."

"Now, now he won't neither," she said quickly, soothingly.

Charlie went softly over to the door and peeped out. "Yonder he comes straight on, kicking the dirt in front," he said.

"Charlie," said his mother, "you go on to Mis' Johnson's and carry them clothes. Maybe your pap wants a word with me. Hurry up," she added nervously.

"I'm—I'm afraid to leave you," he quavered.

"You go on, honey," said Tilsy firmly, "across the field. He'll not hurt your mommee."

The boy finally took up the bag again and went out through the kitchen. Tilsy looked around the room as if searching for some weapon of protection. A heavy step sounded on the porch outside. She ironed faster. Will McNeill, a black, powerful Negro of forty, came just inside the door and stared at Tilsy. His clothes were shabby and dust-stained. Tilsy drew back toward the fire as he entered.

"Well, how's my little girl come on?" he said in a deep growl and came farther into the room. "Don't be skeered. I ain't going to hurt you." His voice was sliding and unctuous and cool.

"We're getting along all right, I reckon," Tilsy finally said.

"Is?" Will laughed. "That's fine. Better'n I am then." He gazed at the walls and furnishings. "Just the same, you don't look like you're flourishing much." He opened the door to the kitchen and stared in. "Hunh, don't look like a millionaire's pantry in there either," he said. "Where's your stove you had last year?"

"I—got rid of it," Tilsy answered evasively.

"I reckon I see that you have," he said sharply and shortly.

"I had to pay Babe's doctor's bill with it," she quavered.

"Babe been sick?" he queried gravely.

"What you care about Babe, well or sick?"

"Look here, none of your sass," snapped Will.

Tilsy lowered her eyes before his threatening gaze. "She was sick most of the winter," she said hurriedly, "and I didn't have no money to pay Dr. Booker, and he said he'd take the stove for payment."

"That damn nigger do that? He ain't no doctor. He's just a humbug with his worm grease and snake fat and sulphur burning."

"He ain't no humbug 'cause he cured Babe." Tilsy was stung to defensiveness.

"Course he cured her," Will flared back. "She'd a-got well anyhow. And he took the stove and left you to cook in that little fireplace—hunh? The old son!" Tilsy trembled but said nothing.

"Listen to me, woman," he went on savagely, "you forgot I helped pay for that stove, ain't you?"

"Yeh," said Tilsy, "you paid five dollars, and I paid fifteen."

"And I'm going to have my five dollars back right now," Will snarled, turning on her. "You cough up that dough hot damn quick."

Tilsy suddenly laughed shrilly and recklessly. "Five dollars! I ain't seen that much money in six months. I ain't, and that's the God's truth."

"Well, you better see it 'fore the next six months come by," Will said sullenly. "That's all I got to say." He stared at her a moment, and then suddenly changed his voice to a gentler tone. "Now look here, girl, let's forget the stove for the present." He put his hand slyly on her hip and stroked it. "How about a little grub? I ain't et no dinner."

Tilsy cringed at his touch. "I ain't either," she said.

"You ain't?"

"What you 'spect me to eat—fire coals and ashes!" she exclaimed almost hysterically.

Will eyed her. "You must be getting low sure enough."

"I ain't had nothing but a cup of thin coffee this whole day. The children didn't have enough to eat for dinner even," she added with sudden and quiet bitterness.

"What you going to do for supper?" he asked, taking a seat.

Tilsy nervously went on ironing. "I sent off after some meal and meat," she finally said.

"Why you keep sucking your teeth?"

Tilsy leaned over the board and answered jerkily, "I got a rising in my jaw. My head's busting open." She cried out, beating her temples with her fists, "I ain't slept none for two nights, and if you don't hush I can't stand it. —Hush I tell you." She turned the garment and ironed faster.

"That's bad," Will said. Then he snapped out, "Say, you ain't playing no tricks on me 'bout being sick, are you?" She made no answer, only rocking her head from side to side. "No, I reckon you're really sick," he finally agreed. "But I'd sorter looked forward to spending the night with you."

Tilsy stopped her ironing and stared at him with wide glinting eyes. "I know what you want—to lay me down on that bed and have your way. But you can traipse right back 'cross the river to your black huzzy over there if you want somebody to lie with."

"Well, I'm going to stay here tonight just the same," said Will determinedly.

"If you do, me'n my children will sleep out in the fields," she cried shrilly.

"Suits me," said Will, lighting his pipe. "But anyhow I've usually had my way when I stopped by here in the past. Maybe I'll have it tonight."

Tilsy's voice hardened. "Before you lay hands on me this night I'll stick my butcher knife in you to the hollow."

"By God, you get riled easy!"

"R-iled easy!" stammered Tilsy. "Will McNeill, I want you to get out'n my house and go back to your old bitch and her passel of puppies."

"Cut out that talk!" he growled threateningly, starting out of his chair.

"Oh, no," said Tilsy with bitter recklessness now, "you can't scare me. I ain't the woman you married them twelve years ago no longer. And I ain't the woman you been coming back to see whenever you felt the sap rising in you. I'm changed, and I hate you worse'n a snake in the grass."

"Hunh, I've heard that spiel before," he said, sitting back and smiling harshly.

"Yeh, yeh, you have," answered Tilsy, her voice cracking. "But I ain't never said it before like that—like I say it now. I've—I've suffered, and I don't care no more. I know what you're coming back for. You want to leave another baby sprouting in me, another baby to tend to and feel fumble and pull and cry through the long nights while you lie rotten with sin and other women." She pointed to the rear door. "If you'll just go out through that door to the forked peach tree back of the house and dig down two feet in the ground, you'll find in a shoe box what you left with me the last time. It was born dead, and it ain't going to happen again"—her voice rose higher—"never so help me God!"

Will stirred uneasily in his chair. "Well, you have had it sorter hard, maybe," he acknowledged unwillingly.

"Hard!" shrilled Tilsy, setting down her iron and holding her jaw in her hand. "Hard! You've killed all the heart I had in me. And me'n my children don't know your name no more." She moved toward him. "And I want you to get off'n this place. Get out'n my house!" she cried. "Get!" He sprung up and held his chair in front of him. "You going?" she demanded, her eyes gleaming.

"You ain't going to run me off that easy," he laughed brutally. "I've invited myself to supper, and I'm gonna stay," and he watched her closely.

"I give you just one minute to hit the grit," moaned Tilsy, her lips tight.

"You better watch them there clothes," warned Will. "Somebody's dress is burning up."

Tilsy turned and snatched the iron from the burning cloth and held up a lacy dress with a great hole burned in it. She stared at it dumbly a moment, then sat down suddenly with her hands clawing at each other in despair. Charlie stuck his head in the door at the left and stood watching Will. Will saw him.

"Is that you, Charlie?" he called kindly. Charlie said nothing. "Don't be so skittish," Will went on. "I ain't wanting to touch you." Charlie laid his piece of meat on the bureau. "Your muh's having just a little sick spell with her head. She'll be all right in a minute." Charlie quietly opened the bureau drawer, and Will called out suspiciously, "Here, boy, you ain't feeling for a gun or something, is you?"

"I'm just going to get out my hooks," said Charlie in a whisper, as he took out a long fishing hook.

Will came up to him. "I dunno," he said, looking suspiciously around at Tilsy. "You all may be up to devilment." Charlie started toward the rear door, but Will grabbed him by the arm. "Nunh-unh, my little man, I saw you when you skeeted across the field. Tell me, did your muh send you to get Mr. Johnson to come drive me off?"

Charlie struggled and began to cry. "Turn me loose! Mom-mee! Mommee!"

"Let that boy alone!" shouted Tilsy, bounding out of her chair.

"Shet your mouth, woman!" roared Will, holding Charlie from the floor by his arm. "If you all think you're driving me off by sending for help, I reckon I'll show you. Speak to me, you little devil, and tell me straight. I'm gonna get at the truth." Charlie suddenly hooked him in the leg. "God Almighty," shrieked Will, "he's stuck me with that fishhook!"

He dropped the boy who darted sobbing under the bed. With groans and twistings Will finally got the hook out of his flesh. His face was distorted with anger as he started toward the bed.

Tilsy screamed, "Don't you bother my boy!" Will got down on his knees and peered under the bed. "I'll kill you before you hurt him!" Tilsy screamed again. But Will began clambering under the bed, ignoring her. Tilsy picked up a chair and brought it down on his back. He rose from the floor and struck her with his fist, sending her tottering across the room.

"I'll—I'll kill that Charlie if I get my hands on him!" he panted. Tilsy flew at him again. He hurled her against the table and then started back under the bed. She seized the hot iron by the holder and sprung toward him. He tried to wrest it from her, but his hand touched it and he yelled with pain. By this time Charlie had crawled out from beneath the bed. Tilsy threw herself wildly at Will. He stumbled backwards over a chair, and then suddenly it was done—she struck him in the head with the iron. He shrieked, staggered, and then dropped limply on the floor, the blood beginning to flow from his face. She brought the iron down on his head again, then dropped it. It rolled into the pile of clothes that had fallen off the bed in the scuffle, and presently a curl of smoke began to rise upward.

"Will! Will!" screamed Tilsy aghast, "Lord-a-mercy, I've killed him!"

She drew away to the rear of the room and sat down on the bed in a daze. Charlie ran to her and clung to her dress, whimpering in fear. And then Sina and Babe came in through the doorway.

"Mommee, we got some meal," Sina called. "And look at the purty flowers Babe picked." Babe held up the flowers. "What's the matter with the man on the floor? Lord, it's Pap!" She and Babe both ran crying to Tilsy, who hugged Babe to her, rocking to and fro.

And rising, she backed out through the rear door, carrying Babe in her arms.

"We got to get help!" she moaned, "we got to get help."

Charlie and Sina followed, holding to her dress and sobbing wildly, and they all went into the fields. The clothes began to burn briskly.

Love at the Hanging

$Y_{es,}$ *child.*

Like a whisper, like a breath, as sudden as death, love can come to you. Something knocks maybe on the door of your heart and says, let me in. And you never know when it's going to knock and when it's not going to knock. So it was the first time I ever laid these two eyes on your grandfather.

I'll never forget the day it happened. What a day! August time it was, and a Friday. A big hanging was being held over there in Hillsborough, and I mean big. Everybody for miles around was up long before the break of day getting primped and dolled and fixed to go to the spectacle. Oh that day! And people, people, white and colored, everywhere! That was the biggest crowd of human beings gathered together I'd ever seen in all my born days. From every direction they came. From the north and the east and the south and the west—in steer carts, in road carts, in wagons, and in carriages. There weren't any automobiles in those days. And the through-trains from the south and the north stopped and unloaded their mergins of folks.

And the University here at Chapel Hill dismissed school that day, because most of the students and professors were planning to go see the hanging.

It sure is a curious thing about the human race, child, curious. Why folks like to congregate like flies around dead things—where ruction and trouble are—is more than I can tell. But they do so now and they did so then. Maybe the sight of grief and pain suffered by others does something to human hearts—makes something sympathetic happen to our souls even. And this wasn't just one hanging with suffering in it. It was three hangings. Three poor sinful men were to be hung by the neck till dead, and "the Lord have mercy on your poor souls," the judge had said.

I knew all three of them. At least I recognized them. Two of them were white men and one of them was a colored man. I knew the colored man well—Louis Colton. And there was Mr. Harris and Mr. Johnson. They were white men, and as full of sin and wickedness as a copperhead snake is full of green poison. Poor Louis. Sorrowful was the day he mixed himself up with those white folks. They were gamblers and drunkards and pistol-toters—robbers and thieves, they were. And when Louis joined up with them, he put himself in their power, everybody said so. And he always did whatever they told him to do. Sam Ragland was in it too. He was another black man but they let him loose because he turned what they called state's evidence.

Yes, child, terrible, terrible it was. But the Good Book says, verily, verily a man shall reap. And all those men sowed trouble and death and they reaped the same in the vineyard of Almighty God. You heard me say many a time, child, if you run with the dogs, you'll scratch fleas. And you heard me say too—when your house is afire, it's too late to dig a well for water to put it out.

Our whole family was all set to go and see the dreadful happening. Up early and breakfast cooked, we soon were dressed in our best bib and tucker, Ma and Pa and the two little boys and we girls. There was a whole carpetful of children in our house. I was the oldest girl in the family and had to keep watch over the little ones. But I'm here to tell you that as soon as we got in the grip of that occasion in Hillsborough they forgot all about me and were scattered and gone, and I forgot all about them too. They left me like chickens leave a duck mother that goes swimming in the water in front of their shocked and troubled eyes. But later on in the day we all re'sembled back at the wagon with no damage done to any of them—except to me, and that wasn't damage, it was love, and it had blossomed in my heart.

The roads were miry and awful then, not like they are now, hard-surfaced and as smooth as an otter's slide and with speeding cars flying on them. And long before we came to the Eno River near the edge of the town the sun was a big blazing ball of fire in the sky and it was 'way up in the morning. Pa whipped up the mule because he felt we were already late. We crossed the bridge and rode on in a jiffy toward the jailhouse on the right hand side there.

And what was the very first thing I saw? It was a big-eyed face looking out of the jail window, and it was nobody's face but poor Louis Colton's. And all wild and sick-looking it was. He saw us and he cried out in a loud voice, "Hey there, you all! This here's Louis!" And without knowing what I was doing, I raised up my hand in a kind of greeting to the poor lost man. But my lips wouldn't say a word. And then he cried out—"This here's the day I'm to be hung, folkses. And I'm jest as clear of what they's hanging me for as ever was Jesus Christ the Lamb of God that taketh away the sins of the world." That was exactly what he said, and I can remember it to this day. My mother grunted and spit a dip of snuff over the wagon into the road. She always did that way suddenly when she was riled.

"That's an awful thing—for him to be telling lies like that and he so close to meeting his Maker," she said.

"I reckon Louis has been reading the Good Book a lot—while he's been shut up in there," said my father, "judging from his words."

It made a crawly feeling at the back of my neck at what poor Louis said and the way his voice sounded and his poor face looked.

"Well," my mother said as she looked around at us children, "mark my word that a gap in the ax always shows in the chips. And, children, listen to what I say—a minute may break what an eternity of time can never heal."

"That's so," said my father, "and that's why we brought you over here—so every one of you can learn a lesson—a lesson to go with you through life. And you needn't worry about Louis Colton, you needn't cry lost tears for him. He was guilty. He's got to suffer for it. He split that good white woman's head open with an ax."

"Amen," said my mother, "and it was proved on him. And another thing he did. Don't forget that," she added.

Love at the Hanging

"I'm not," said my daddy. "Louis put strychnine and ar-
senic in his wife's coffee, children, and he killed her too. But
they never did convict him of that, though certainly everyone
knew he did it. But sure she was a black woman."

"Sure they did," said Mother. "But when he came to
killing that white woman—that professor's wife and she finding
him robbing her house—well, that's where he spilled hot coffee
all over himself."

"Didn't he though," said my daddy.

And now the people were crowding all around the jailhouse like a swarm of bees. And my daddy drew up close by
and let us get out, and he went off and hitched the mule to a tree
in the jailhouse yard. And there we children all stood around in
the push of people looking on with great big sorrowful eyes and
waiting to see the prisoners brought out.

Soon here came the High Sheriff and his deputies in their
big boots—clonk-clonk, and they were carrying their pistols in
their hands. And they went in the jail and brought out the
prisoners handcuffed. And the scattering dogs around began to
bark. The people stretched and craned and gaped to see it all.
And the deputies walked the three of them around in the yard,
the three that were to die, to let them partake and taste the
sunshine and the sweet air for their last day on earth.

And any time now, child, that I close my eyes, I can see
their sick faces. And death was in them and their eyes were
wide-rimmed and red. The white men had beards on their faces
and behind it all you could see their skin was as white as Sunday
sheets. And poor Louis's eyes were smoky and hollow and
turning in their sockets like he couldn't help himself. And his
mouth stayed open all the time, like a man feeling about to
vomit. And he kept dripping and drooling, and every once in a
while he'd raise up his sleeve and wipe the spittle away from his
chin.

Oh, how my heart ached to see it all! And I squeezed little
Eulalie's hand so hard she cried. And Ma pulled her away from
me. "Stop hurting that child," she said.

Then Mr. Harris, the white man, stopped walking around
and held up his two cuffed hands, and everybody got silent the
way you do in the graveyard when the preacher holds up his

hand ready to start saying, "Ashes to ashes and dust to dust."
Then the poor man began to preach loud and strong to all the
people. He told them about his evil and wicked ways and how
he'd repented of all his sins and how everybody ought to take
warning from what his life had turned out to be—so that they
might escape the wrath of God the Saviour and such woe and
terrible damnation in the end of their days.

And while he went on talking a lot of people began to cry
like at a revival meeting. I cried myself. I couldn't help it. Later it
was told that a number of folks got religion that day and led
better lives henceforth, one of them being old Hezekiah Faulkner.
He was a lowdown white man, liquor seller, and sinful creature.
It was said he was the one who sold Louis the liquor regularly,
and he furnished the white men with it too. And no doubt the
liquor had something to do with their evil doings. Anyhow my
daddy said it would be just as well if old Hezekiah got his
hanging along with Louis and the others, for Louis as a matter of
fact was drunk on old Hezekiah's liquor the very night he killed
the good white woman.

But Hezekiah didn't get his grace there in front of the
jailhouse. He was too tough for that. It was only when he saw
later what happened up on the hill—when he saw the bodies
hanging there—that the lesson written in their deaths came
home to him. Forty years the preachers had been after his moss-
backed soul and couldn't change him. But that hanging reached
him all right, and he later joined the church. And it reached into
the souls of plenty of others too. Yes, child, it did.

It was getting mighty close to the middle of the day and
lunchtime now. Most everyone had brought a midday snack,
but nobody was eating it. The folks were waiting for the hanging. And besides they felt sort of weak in the stomach and didn't
have much appetite. Pretty soon here came a wagon rattling up,
pulled along by a big white mule and driven by a fat red-headed
boy. And in that wagon were three black coffins, made of pine
planking no doubt and covered with black cheese cloth. The
people drew back from in front of it like it had been a hearse or
the horse of death itself come from Satan and the world beyond.
The sheriff and the deputies took hold of the prisoners and

helped them trembling up into the wagon. And with the guards walking along, the wagon started on up through the town toward Gallows Hill.

And while the wagon rolled along and all of us kept following after it, and the dogs too, there Mr. Harris stood up in it with one knee leaning on his own coffin to balance himself, and he kept on preaching and giving advice to the people. And poor Louis broke into a song, singing it all by himself. I knew that song the way a lot of other people did, and I've never forgotten it from that day to this. And every time they sing it in White Rock Church I think about that hanging. And when you hear it, child, you think about it too. Yes, you better—

> *The lightning flares, the thunders roll,*
> *The earthquake shakes from pole to pole—*
> *Oh, Jesus Christ, my living God,*
> *Make up my dying bed.*

And soon most of the folks had joined in with the singing. But my daddy and my mother didn't sing. They were strong hard-shell folks. And up through the town we all marched.

> *The rocks and hills melt with the sun*
> *And man and all his works are done.*

And the wheels kept knocking under the weight of the men loaded in that wagon, knocking as if in time with the song. And rocking in my chair many a time since, I've heard it knock, knock in my remembrance. Finally we mounted up to Gallows Hill on the north edge of the town. And there the scaffold was already built with new boards and scantling and three new looped ropes hanging down, waiting all in a row. The boy stopped the wagon by the scaffold, and the sheriff and the guards helped the prisoners down and led them up the little steps. The three of them stood there and the sheriff took the handcuffs off of them while the guards held their arms, and then he tied their hands behind them. And all the while each one was looking through the noose that was right in front of his face. And they were all meek as little children.

The Reverend A. C. Dixon, the big white Chapel Hill preacher, mounted the steps to preach. You've heard me tell about him, child. He later went across the ocean to preach before the king. Well, Reverend Dixon mounted up on the scaffold, and he put his hand gently on each of the men. And he kept his hand longest on Louis's shoulder, like maybe he felt more sorry for him. Then he turned around, opened up his Bible and took his text—"When I would do good, evil is present with me."

More than an hour he preached to the crowd on how pride goeth before destruction and a haughty spirit before a fall, and in such an hour as you know not the Son of Man cometh. Yes, he said, be sure a man's sins will be found out, for there is no hiding place from the wide watching eye of God.

And everybody in that vast throng of people hung on his words, drinking them in. But the poor prisoner criminals kept standing there, twisting about every now and then on their tired feet like they wished he'd hush and get it over and done with.

And when finally the sermon was finished, the preacher led in a long prayer. And all over the hillsides and up in the trees people sat and stood. Their heads were bowed like weeping willow trees. Then at the end of the prayer, Reverend Dixon said, "Our Father who art in heaven," and the hundreds and thousands of people, white and black, joined in the Lord's Prayer just like children in the church on Sunday. And the poor fellows on the scaffold standing there with their heads bowed, they did so too and so did the sheriff and the guards. Clean across the town and out into the country rolled the great reciting voices of sound, saying "Lead us not into temptation but deliver us from evil, for thine is the kingdom and the power and the glory, forever and ever, Amen."

Everybody in that vast and mighty multitude was feeling sorrowful and forgiving now. My own heart ached like it couldn't stand but a little bit more, and I could just feel that everybody else's heart was aching and filled with sorrow too. And so much sorrow was everywhere that forgiveness was in all our hearts. Kindness was in people's souls, one to another, and especially toward the poor condemned ones about to die. And here and there and all round about weeping and sobbing began breaking out. Nobody felt like hanging anybody now. Everybody was sorry such an awful thing was to be. But still every last one of us knew that the hanging must be. For the law said hang and the law, child, take it from me, is an all-powerful and fearsome thing. Remember that.

The pure tears were stinging and blinding my eyes, and I turned away from the sad sight on the scaffold. There right across from me was a young man looking off, and there were some water drops on his cheeks also. I looked at him, and he looked around at me—in the dimness of our tears we saw each other, and my heart was swelling so with grief I felt close to him, though he was a stranger, and I fully believed he felt close to me too. I put my handkerchief to my mouth to keep from crying aloud.

Then I heard the great preacher saying a few low kind words to each of the prisoners. I couldn't understand what he was saying, but I knew he was comforting them. And in the midst of it all Louis suddenly shouted out in a loud voice that could be heard clean across the Eno River. "This day certain to my soul—I'm goan be with Jesus in Paradise. Yea, in the arms of my loving Saviour—that's where I'm goan be this day!"

And from the hillsides and from the little slopes and gullies where the people were crowded, you could hear scattered amens and bless you, brother. And the dogs started barking again.

Next the sheriff and the guards stepped up and put black smothering caps on all three of them, and there they stood with those black things on them looking like three booger bears or serenaders to scare the daylights out of you on Christmas night— or maybe like the Ku Klux Klan creatures too.

While they were doing this, Reverend Dixon reached up his hands high and started a song, leading the people in a great hymn anthem. We sing it in our church still to this day—

> *Who is this that comes from far*
> *With his garments dipped in blood,*
> *Stray triumphant traveler*
> *Is he man or is he God?*

Then all of a sudden as if God the Saviour had made answer back, there came from deep beneath the earth to the west a shaking growl and rumble of great thunder. People looked all about them, at one another. It seemed like there was a sign in it or something, for we had just been singing when we came marching up the hill about the thunder rolling from pole to pole.

The thunder put a stop to the singing in the crowd. The preacher went on a few lines further and then only he and Louis were singing. The song coming out from under that black cap gave everybody the shivers, I tell you. The ropes were now put around the necks of the three lost souls. The sheriff raised his hand in a sign, and right at that very moment the thunder crashed deep and frighteningly once more. A trembling ran all through the people and I could feel it. Everybody could feel it, feel that there was something wrong with the happenings of this day. And it was like the great voice of the Almighty from far down under the earth was speaking out against it.

And all the while everybody put their eyes on the men on the scaffold. I can still see them standing a little knee-bent there. And I was thinking when the thunder sounded about that other old song we used to sing there in White Rock—

> *Day of wrath, O day of mourning*
> *See fulfilled the prophet's warning.*

And I looked up and the young stranger had moved nearer to me now, and it seemed just as natural as could be that he had done so. I felt like moving toward him too, and maybe I did take a step or two and didn't know it. Now I could see far to the west and beyond the sycamores along Eno River and the chestnut oaks on top of Occoneechee Mountain a great roll of rushing clouds coming on up over the world there like the Judgment Day itself.

A lump was in my throat and a kind of sick feeling in my stomach. And my mouth kept filling with spittle and I wanted to spit it out. But a girl wasn't supposed to. I turned away so the young stranger wouldn't see me and wiped my mouth on my sleeve just the way poor Louis had been doing.

And I looked back at the scaffold and I knew Louis couldn't wipe his mouth now because his hands were tied behind him. And it didn't make any difference anyhow, for the black cap was over his face and maybe that would soak it up like bread does gravy.

The sheriff dropped his hand, and the guard standing below on the ground and behind a plank handle reached out and pulled the handle easy-like with his hand. The props flew out like dynamite had hit them. Down fell the trap doors and the men shot through them like rocks you might drop into a creek, and the preacher jumped back as if he was afraid he might fall through too.

At that second, the very second the handle was pulled and the prisoners fell there came one of the awfulest ripping and tearing crashings of lightning down from the sky that I'd ever experienced. People screamed and shouted and jumped and turned round and round. And a great moaning mumble rose from the multitude. And the dogs just about went wild—going away from there. And that lightning had struck a big oak tree just over the brow of the hill, and smoke and brimstone could be seen going up the sky where it had struck.

Yes, child, it was just as if the Lord that makes the heavens and the earth and holds them in the hollow of his hand—just as if he had spoken with the thunderbolt of his own voice, saying, oh human race, the shame and pity of what you're doing!

And the wiggling of the three men on the rope began to stop. I couldn't look at them but I knew they were wiggling and I could hear the creaking of the scaffold, the creaking becoming less and less. And I looked at the people while they gazed at the scaffold, and I could read in the countenance of their faces what was happening, especially the young stranger where he kept swallowing by his Adam's apple to keep from crying as he saw the dreadful sight.

Then everything got still as death. There was no movement,

no noise from all the people, no sound in the air. There was no more lightning nor thunder now. After a minute or two an easy little wind began blowing like a sort of blessing over the scene. A light easy wind it was. Then with a roar and flooding spatter the rain came—coming across the land like the trampling of a flock of goats. It struck the crowd in a great gust. I could hear the drops plop-plopping on the scaffold planking and on the shirts of the three bodies hanging from their ropes. And all of a sudden I was struck by a worry about them hanging there helpless and getting wet, and maybe they'd catch their death of cold. Just for a second I was.

Then the people seemed to wake up, the douse of cold rain falling on them woke them up and brought them back out of the spell of all the terrible happenings. And they started scattering in all directions like biddies before a hawk, professors, students, everybody.

I took a last quick look back toward the scaffold. There were the three pitiful men hanging all wet and bedraggled and their necks stretched out nearly half as long as your arm, like a chicken's neck when you pull it to break it.

Then I turned really sick and I whirled around looking for my mother, and I sprang quickly to run away from there and bam, I banged right into the young stranger, who was standing there in front of me. And he put out his arm good and strong and he held me up. I was shaking and quivering and about to cry. I looked up at him and he didn't drop his arm, but he kept looking at me and I at him. And I was sobbing loudly now. And he smiled at me. All of a sudden, child, I didn't want to run away anymore. All of a sudden I was forgetting about the hanging. I wanted him to keep his arm around me and hold me up, and he did. He kept looking in my eyes and I looked in his, and his arm was strong about me.

Then I turned away and he walked along with me, helping me through the crowd. And my heart was beginning to sing. And it all was so sudden but just as natural as life. Grief and woe in our two hearts had made it so—making it so we came toward each other, reaching toward each other. There's an old saying—true love's the weft of life, but it sometimes comes through a sorrowful shuttle.

And that's how I first met your grandpa. Yes, child—all on account of the hanging. And that's how come you got into this world. If I hadn't met him—um!—

Nello

~~~~~~

*Y*esterday after a long bout with the flu I was able to be up and about the house. I felt weak and no 'count. I decided to go into town in the April weather, mail some letters and maybe get a shave and massage to make me feel better.

My usual barber was sitting in his chair reading the funnies. He got up lazily yet resolutely as I entered, laid his paper aside, and picked up his voluminous barber cloth.

"Come right in, come right in, Doc," he said cheerily.

I took off my coat, hung it up, loosened my shirt collar, and turned toward the waiting restful chair.

"What'll it be, Doc?" And with both hands he gave the cloth a few wide popping flaps in the air.

"A shave and a good massage," I said as I sat down.

"Right, right as rain," he said. "Make you feel better."

He lowered the chair flat back and spread the cloth over me and began tucking it in around my neck. "You look kind of peaked, Doc," he said.

"Yeah, I've been laid up with the flu," I said.

"Bad stuff—flu," he said.

I lay looking up at the heavy fluorescent light fixture hanging directly and threateningly above. Heavy!

"How've you been?" I said.

"Okay, okay," he answered. "Everything quiet." And then his always shattering laugh broke the air. "Nothing ever happens in a barbershop—nothing." Some of the other barbers laughed too.

"Yeah," I said, "a good place to watch life go by, through the window there."

"Sir?"

"I say a good place to watch things pass—out on the street there."

"Yeah, out of the corner of your eye, you might say."

He began stropping his razor.

"A shine too," I said.

"Hey, boy! A shine over here!" He snapped on the lather mixer. I lay relaxed. It whirred. I closed my eyes. Already I felt better. Now he slip-slopped the creamy soap foam on my cheeks and chin. He began to rub pressingly.

Outside on the sidewalk the tapping of women's heels went along. I heard it, visualized a bit, and caught the passing mixture of young people's voices—Easter shoppers, elated, expectant, generous. Christ is risen—the fish are biting!

Now hot towels and more soap foam. This was good. I thought of my wife visiting in Boston, wondered how things were going with her and the children there. I'd be glad when she got back.

"How's that feel?" the barber said.

"Fine," I mumbled.

A bit more razor-stropping. And then the shaving began. Suddenly a strong and new hand lifted my foot and put it up on the shine last. I looked out on the incline to speak to Nello as usual, but I saw a stranger, an intense square-cut wide-nostrilled young mulatto face, not Nello at all with his wild razor scars and his shifting restless yellow-balled eyes—Nello, friend to me and my shoes these long times gone.

"You've got a new man," I finally said to the barber.

"Yeah, yeah, Doc, we have."

"How's Nello getting along?" I asked.

He shaved on a while and the strong new hands applied polish on my shoes. I was being well looked after, top and bottom. Good.

"Yes," the barber said presently, and I felt him wipe the razor on the swatch of paper-roll across my breast. "His name's Early. Say, Early, fix 'Fessor's shoes up right, boy. Fix 'em up." He spoke with good and soul-breezy authority.

"Yessuh," I heard Early's bright answer. I felt him rubbing the cleaning cloth heavily and enclosingly around my shoe.

"Yeah, he's new," the barber went on, "but he'll learn. The razor feel all right?"

"Sure."

He concentrated on his job. The left side now that the right was done, and then the upper lip, carefully, tiny, furtive scrapings, and on into the corners of the mouth. Next under the jowls and the chin, and then slip and up under the lower lip. Again the razor was wiped.

"How's Nello getting on?" I asked, breathing a bit more freely.

No answer. "Turn Doctor's pants up, boy, or you'll get that blacking on 'em," he said to Early.

"Yessuh," said Early quickly. I felt him fumble about my ankle. Next he was finishing with the paste on this shoe and was polishing away, now and then trying to make his shine cloth pop, but without success. Not the way Nello could do it. Nello could make the train sound of old Ninety-seven coming around the bend—whoo-whoo, he could really play his railroad tune with that cloth.

Then a dampening soft palm-smearing with warm water and a quick second going-over with the razor.

"Feel better now?"

"Yeah, a lot."

"Good."

Next three hot towels in succession and then the massaging cream—long squeezing palm strokes, half-brutal, half-caressing.

"That'll take some of the tension out."

"Yup—oom—uh," I answered under his hand-butt glides.

"You been working hard, Doc?"

"Oh, so-so."

"Writing more plays?" And again his laugh shattered the air. I wondered some.

"Well, trying, I guess," I mumbled.

"Soon be time to open up your outdoor dramas again, won't it?"

"Yeah. Time goes by in a hurry."

"Don't it? The older you get the faster it goes. Getting so now seem like I can hear the Sunday papers falling in front of my gate one 'pon top of the other." Again he laughed and I could feel him looking about the barbershop to his fellows with his merry bright blue eyes.

"Yes, and don't the birthdays come fast?"

Rub, rub, rub. "They do." Silence—rub, rub. "Yeh, Nello won't be with us any more," he finally spoke up, quietly, coldly even, without interest, a simple reply to a question remembered.

"He won't?"

"No."

"Too bad," I said, thinking of the long absences in the past when Nello was away on the chain gang serving time for drunkenness, for fighting. Nello!

And now Early's rough untrained hand laid the finished foot spasmodically up on the foot rest of the barber chair, shifted his last around, grabbed the other foot and stuck it awkwardly down and began scraping at it with the butt of his brush. How different from the feel of Nello's long expert fingers!

"I guess you finally got worn out with him," I said.

The barber pushed down and palmed up the drying cream, cleaning out the dirty and oily pores.

"This is a new kind of cream—really does the work," he said.

"Up—oom—no doubt," I mumbled.

"He was good at shining shoes what time he was sober—Nello, I mean. That's why we kept him on," he said.

"Yeah, he was a good sort of fellow all the same."

"He was and he wasn't. Never could tell what was on his mind. Never talked much."

"Not much," I said. "I noticed that."

And I lay remembering the hard crisp calls of the different barbers in the shop—"Hey, boy, shine 'em up here. Brush here, boy. Make it snappy. Can't wait all day"—these calls and orders of times past. And I could see Nello's flying hands, his quick movements, his extended palm for the coin, the whisk broom under his arm, his bows, his masklike scarred face, the yellow-balled eyes—the deep brown pupils that looked at you and didn't look at you—the deep brown pupils smoky and, yes, sightless in their seeing—or what did they see?

"He was mean when he got full of that old wine," said the barber now brushing away the dirty crumbs of cream from my face.

"Is he back on the roads again?"

"He may be for all I know," and he laughed his shattering laugh once more. "Yeh, if they've got a chain gang in yonder world."

A tremor went through me. "Why? What's happened to Nello?"

The easing hot towel again now and then another.

"Too hot?"

"Noo-unh."

"Just right?"

"Uhm—yes."

"I know from times past you like 'em hot. Now Dr. Rankin likes 'em hot too, says they make him ready to face the day. Every morning he's in here, the first customer of all." He called to the next barber in the row. "Has Dr. Rankin ever missed a day, do you remember?"

"Not a day," Joe answered. "Not so far as I remember, except Sunday and we're closed on Sunday. Hah! Hah!"

"Hah! Hah!" said my barber.

The towel was lifted now and rubbing, slow, long, seductive, not rough now, not at all, soothing, sweet, like a woman's tender loving. I wondered how she was doing in Boston. She'd be home soon.

These hands were not so sweet, not so soothing as they should be now. Something. A worry. Nello—my bruised and lost and wordless friend. Nello.

"You ain't been in lately," the barber queried and announced half-accusingly.

"No."

"Been on the puny list—you say?"

"Yeah, sort of—been away too."

"Yeh, working at your outdoor plays?"

"Some."

"You hadn't heard 'bout Nello. He conked out—croaked, I mean."

"What?"

"Yeh, up and died last week."

"Good gracious!" I half sat up as if that would help, then lay back again. "Too bad, too bad." My words were foolish, said to myself.

"I don't know. Had it coming to him, I reckon."

"How you mean?"

"That old wine and stuff. Runs 'em crazy, burns up their liver."

"Take a lot of that twelve percent stuff to kill a man," I answered a little sharply.

"It all depends. Want some witch hazel, 'Fessor?"

"Yes, oh yes. Anything."

"Mighty good for the tender face. And you're sort of tender down around your Adam's apple."

Next the stinging cool and scented lotion. "Been scraping yourself kind of close down there, ain't you?"

"Yeah. But Nello—"

"Gone."

"Goodness! He was a young fellow."

"Can't always tell about a nigger. They can look young and still be old—like Chinamen."

"How old was he?"

"Say—" and he called down the line of barbers, "fellows, 'Fessor wants to know how old Nello was."

"Ayeh," said Joe the barber near at the right. And he snickered and I could hear his razor popping as he slapped the strap in boyish braggadocio.

"Oh, about forty," another barber down the line called.

"He was forty-two next April fourteen," said Early. And he spoke softly and for my ears only. But my barber heard him.

"Hey, what do you know?" he called crowingly. "Early here said Nello would a-been forty-two next April."

"Brush here, boy," called a barber down the line. Early laid my foot up finished and sprang away. Now the cool dry final towel, smelling of the heat of the laundry, like the sheets my mother used to dry on chairs before the wood fire on rainy days long ago, enwrapped my face.

"It was roaches of the liver got him," said the barber. "He was plumb et up with it. Didn't know it either. Worked right up to the last. He come in here to work a-Wednesday morning and he was dead Thursday, the next day. Some the fellows said to him, 'Nello, you're moving mighty slow today'—that was Wednesday—'Nello, make it snappy,' we would tell him. And old Nello would mumble something 'bout not feeling so good. 'Reckon I ort to see a doctor,' he said long about quitting time."

"That old wine," said Joe, the barber at the right. "Roaches of the liver—yeh. My granddaddy went like that. The doctor said his liver was about the size of an orange and hard as a hickory nut."

"Yeh," said my barber, "it'll kill you—booze will. Powder, 'Fessor?"

"No—yes, powder, a little."

Then the dab, dab, pat, pat of the end-folded towel. Sweet stuff. Mennen's.

"Thanks."

"We heard about it later. His sister come in here to get his last wages. Friday that was. He was already dead."

"Too young to die. A pity." Foolish words I spoke again!

The barber slammed his foot on the chair pedal and swung me sitting up. His hands wiggled and dug into my scalp. "Your hair's mighty dry, Doc. Some lanolin? Make you feel better."

"All right."

"Good for the scalp." Then came his smearing and rubbing. Next a hot towel was wound around my head like a Hindu's turban. I thought of Conan Doyle's story, "The Speckled Band," with the snake coiled on the head of the dead Dr. Roylott. "Seems Nello got home and went to bed Wednesday," my barber went on. "Then the doctor come—Doctor Jordan it was. He examined him and saw he was already half-dead. 'I got to get you to the hospital,' he said. And he left him. Sure puts a shine on your hair, this sheep's grease does." And he brushed and brushed and combed and combed.

"Did they get him to the hospital?"

"Well, yes—the next day—Thursday."

And all night Nello lying in his ragged bed, looking at

what, thinking of what? He never would talk much. Now the barbers are stropping their razors, winking and jibing—Been with that old wine again, eh, Nello? Ninety days.again. Now the bark of the convict boss—Lift that pick—heigh you—swing on it—roll that Georgia buggy, boy—tell the news—make your time—make it sweet and low.

"The next day Doc come, as I say," said the barber, "Thursday morning. They go in to wake Nello, and no waking." Again I felt the brush, brush, the comb, comb, and brush, brush again. "Your hair is standing up in a sort of cowlick here, 'Fessor, where you been sleeping on it. I'll get it down in a minute. He was already in a coma—lying there, his sister said, scarcely breathing at all. They started with him in the ambulance. Yeah, in a stooper he was and he was dead when they got to the ambulance entrance at Memorial Hospital. Well, there you are, Doc."

The cloth was unpinned, a bit of air-hosing inside my collar followed, and I stepped from the chair. I tied my tie, and Early helped me on with my coat and brushed me industriously off. I paid my barber and I gave Early a little extra.

"Feel better, Doc?" said the barber as he crashed the cash register open.

"Yeah, better!"—I almost shouted the words, then I softed them down as I saw his eyes flare. "You've fixed me up fine."

"Come again, 'Fessor."

"Yeah. Where did they bury Nello?"

"Wanter see his grave, 'Fessor?"

I heard two or three of the other barbers laugh. They knew me, they knew me of old.

"I just wanted to find out."

"Out in the country somewhere. Heigh, any you fellows know where they buried Nello?" And none of them did.

"They buried him at Antioch Church," said Early almost too softly for me to hear. I gave him a grateful look.

"How long did Nello work here for you folks?" I said.

"Oh, ten, fifteen years maybe—off and on," said the barber. "And all the time that old wine, that old wine business. We were mighty patient with Nello."

"I see," I said.

Going out I let the door slam hard. And as I walked on I could hear my barber saying to his fellows, in my mind I could hear it, "What's the matter with 'Fessor? Seem like he went off kinder mad or sump'n—let the door slam like that."

"Can't tell about these writing fellows," said Joe the near-by barber.

"Next!" my barber called.

Frizzle

~~~~~~

In the old days there lived a great Negro preacher in our Little
Bethel neighborhood, and he was a bohunkus and plumb devil
on wheels, so the story went. Yessir, he was a bad actor all right,
bad as they make 'em. But the people didn't know about it till
later when this business about Frizzle came out. The Negroes
were awed to death of him though, for they felt that he was such
a mighty man of God and worker in the vineyard and they were
so weak and sinful themselves. When he'd come up on a neighbor's porch at night, the people would shake in their beds, and
they'd rise mighty quick to let him in and get down cold as it
might be in their drawers and nightgowns and have a word of
prayer for their lost and undone condition. After he'd prayed
and maybe cleaned out the pantry he'd go away. Of course
sometimes he'd spend the night and nobody could sleep in the
house hardly for his snores shaking the windows. And it was
whispered about that if there was any good-looking brown girls
in that house, they'd better keep their doors barred and their
drawers on tight. And then on Sunday at church time, Lord,
how he'd freeze the very hearts of the congregation in their
bosoms with his loud sermons about hell-fire and the weeping
and wailing and gnashing of teeth that was ahead of them when
they might be coming up before the judgment bar of Almighty
God.

Well, that's the kind of fellow he was. And everywhere for
miles around, up from Silver Run, down from Macneill's Ferry,
he drove the Negroes into the fold. And every Sunday they were
bowed down in falling rows at the mourners' bench. Finally, so
it was said, old Satan got so disgusted he quit visiting in the

neighborhood, for everybody was good by that time and sinful deeds were scarcer than hens' teeth. And there were a lot of sanctified disciple people scattered about. But that preacher weren't sanctified as they later found out.

Now this old black rapscallion had a poor little wife and two little boys, and the three of them were smart as honeybees in pear blossom time. Up early they were and to bed late, and hard work was their middle name. Every day they'd grub roots down in the newground or hoe the corn or pick the cotton or peas till the ends of their little fingers would drip blood. Yessiree.

But did that preacher care? Not him. And he weren't never satisfied either, not him. Nothing ever suited him. And he never thanked 'em, he didn't, no matter how hard they worked. And he never bought 'em any little gifts at Christmas time nor any other time, for he studied 'bout nothing but himself and what he called his God. And mostly 'bout himself no doubt. These little boys were named Paul and Silas, and they were so ragged and pitiful and thin it'd make your heart strike sorrow to glimpse 'em in the cold frosty fields of morning. And the little wife was thin and ragged and pitiful likewise too. I don't know what her name was, but they called her Mammy. And so they worked day after day, month after month for their mighty lord and master, this old rapscallion.

I want you to realize that that preacher took all the good things to eat himself and all the warm clothes to wear, because as he said Old Moster's work was most important and he needed all the strength he could summons to push forward in His holy name. Seems like the good King in the sky wouldn't let such a bad man be out doing his work, don't it? But still you never know. Maybe all that time the Lord—or whoever He is—had something up his sleeve.

And whenever that preacher got mad—be dag, they said it was same as if brimstone and blue lightning had struck where you stood. And if the little woman and the boys happened to forget maybe and raise a peep around the house and him reading his Bible, he'd fly out at 'em like a sore-tailed cat and frail 'em with the flam of his hand. Yes sir, everybody'd better stay quiet, they had, while he communed with himself and pondered on his sermons. So come day, go night, rainfall or shine, they got more and more scared of him and pitifuller and sadder and thin. But they never complained, and whatever he told 'em to do they'd do it quick as life would let 'em.

Now these little boys had something they loved better than breath itself, and that was their dog named Frizzle—an old stray critter that had taken up at their house for the lack of any place to go. Nobody explained why the preacher let the boys keep that dog, but maybe the Devil himself sometime can't help doing at least one good thing. And besides, maybe the preacher thought Frizzle would make a sort of watchdog, help keep away the ha'nts and other things that might pester him in the night.

Like most Negroes' dogs, of course, Frizzle weren't really worth the powder and shot 'twould take to kill her, but the boys thought she was the rose of Sharon and bright and morning star. They doted on her, took care of her and cherished her the way a girl child does her doll baby. At night sometimes when it was cold and the preacher was dead asleep, they'd slip out and get the old long-haired thing from under the house and let her sleep in the bed with them. And every morning Frizzle would go with them into the newground or the corn or cotton patch and lie right there under a pea vine or sassafras bush and snooze till they were through work and then come home with 'em at dark when day was done.

One night that preacher come back with a sheep in his buggy some of the good folks had give him at a pounding. That was the way they did things in the old days, black and white. The good sisters and brothers would bring a pound of things or more to give their preacher in place of money. And they called that a pounding. So that's how he got the sheep. And he told the little wife to shut it up in a pen and fatten it, and one of these days they'd have a big meal. Along in the fall was going to be a big 'sociation time and then they'd have plenty of mutton for the gathering.

So she and the little boys went down to the creek below the house and got some planks and pieces of scantling had been washed up there by the big freshet, and toted 'em home with might and main. They scratched out some nails from around the washpot where naily boards had been burned, and with a rock for a hammer they built a little pen near the yard and put that sheep in it. And every day after that they'd feed it bits of cornbread and collards. And the little boys would go off and pull crab grass and weeds from the fence jambs and the ends of the row for it. So in time it fattened up some whilst they all kept waiting for the day when they'd have a mess of mutton. The truth is I don't reckon it ever did get very fat. Anyway 'twas said the company complained that it weren't so fat the night they came for the big meal.

Well, one morning about first frost time, the preacher got up and told the woman he was going off to the big conference and 'sociation meeting over at Cedar Grove Church and that the day had come for her to kill that sheep, being he'd run his hand over it and it was fat enough. "Roast it up brown and dandy," he said, "for today is really the day and certain to my soul tonight three big preachers will surely be here to partake under our humble rooftree." And with that he drove off flailing his spavined one-eyed Madge mule, in a hurry to get to the big doings. The poor little woman sat around for a while, and then got the butcher knife and whetted it up on a hunk of grindstone. The little boys sat around too and watched her as she whetted whee-ah, whee-ah away, their eyes bright and eager as new buttons. Then when she'd got a hair edge on the knife, she and the two of them went out to the pen to kill the sheep.

Of course Frizzle was there too, watching everything and wagging her old draggly tail. Maybe she knew what was going to happen to that sheep and wanted to be in on it. Maybe she could already see scraps for herself. The little woman reached into the pen and caught the sheep by the ear and drew back the butcher knife to deal the death blow to its throat. But just as she brought the knife swoosh around and under, old Frizzle barked and made a lunge at the fence, trying to help out. The sheep reared back and the knife only slitted the edge of her goozle.

And now with a loud baa-baa that sheep flirted and jumped and jerked loose from the woman, and quick as a flash busted right out of the rotten pen and went running down the hill slope into the thick woods at the bottom, the blood going drip-drap out of the gash in its neck. The little woman went running after it, hollering for it to come back, co-sheepy, co-sheepy, come back. But it kept right on, bouncing from one side to the other like it was trying to dodge something, and its tail jiggling up and down the way lambs do when they're sucking their mammy. And the dog Frizzle went running after it too, yelping for every breath and snipping at the sheep's legs, which made it run all the faster. The two little boys tore along behind, but they were so small they were soon left out of sight. Then when little Paul stumped his toe bad and started bawling, the two of 'em stopped and waited for Mammy to catch the sheep herself.

Now that little old woman being so terrible afraid of the preacher, as I told you, knew she was bound to catch that sheep or maybe like as not get her brains beat out when he come home, and he might kill her. So she and Frizzle went on trotting along for two hours through the woods, but they couldn't find that sheep. Way down in the deep thickets of the swamp she finally ran out of breath and set down on a log there with the butcher knife in her hand crying and wondering what in the world she was going to do. She could already see her mighty husband coming home with the three other preachers. And how he would stomp into the house, call out in his loud voice to serve up the supper! And there wouldn't be any supper. No doubt, she could almost feel the knuckles of his big hand against her jaw, the one she had so much toothache in. One minute maybe she wished she could keep on through the woods and never go back, and then maybe she thought of the two boys, and if she could only take them and fly away like a bird somewhere and hide. But the way the song said, "There ain't no hiding place."

And while she sat there thinking and her heart all choked up with the misery inside her, she heard faithful Frizzle barking a time or two on the trail a few yards ahead. So she rose up and staggered on. Somehow she had to have that roast ready to serve tonight. Somehow—but at that minute Frizzle came out of the thicket carrying one of them little speckled land terrapins in her mouth, and stood looking at Mammy and wagging her tail hopelessly, as much as if the sheep had got away for good and here was the next best thing. "Sic 'em, Frizzle, sic 'em," the little woman whimpered trying to urge the dog on after the sheep. But Frizzle had had enough running for that day, and dropping the terrapin she went over to a bed of dry leaves by a log and lay down. And the little old woman sat down on the log and began to stroke old Frizzle's hair. And she thought and thought.

The little boys up on the hill waited around for an hour or two, fearful and horrified at what might happen to Mammy if she didn't catch that sheep. By this time Paul had stopped his crying, for Silas had tied up his hurt toe with a piece of his ragged shirt and he felt better. And besides, the deep worry about Mammy had taken his mind off his own troubles. What in the world could they do to help her out? Sure Pappy might— Then suddenly joy broke in their two little loyal hearts, for there was Mammy coming out into the clearing, and she was struggling along with something wrapped in her apron. Yes, it was the sheep. She had already killed and skinned it there in the woods.

"You ketched it, you ketched it, Mammy," they shrieked almost beside themselves, as they hurried to meet her.

"I got it," she called out, half giggling and half crying, and still panting from her great running.

"Good Mammy, good Mammy," said little Silas, patting her on the hip.

"Us knowed you'd ketch it, Mammy," little Paul chirped, as he limped and padded along beside her.

"Yes," she kept saying, "yes." Then she told them to go into the house and build a fire in the stove. The little boys run fast as they could to do what she told 'em, for they were tickled and pleased that the sheep had been ketched and now Pappy wouldn't beat Mammy and hurt her and make her moan in the night, and they lying shivering and afraid on their shuck mattresses in the shed.

All the rest of that day they cooked the roast. Paul and Silas were busy as little Trojas men, working around the stove, keeping the fire going and bringing in dry sticks and limbs from the woods. And they went out into the garden too and got a lot of sage leaves and onions and red pepper to season it up with.

Along about dark sure enough here come that great black preacher rolling in behind his old Madge mule and three other brethren were with him, all hungry as famished varmints. And there was howdy-doings, hallelujahs, and a loud scramble of holy talk as they left the buggy and took possession of the premises. The two boys would have to put the mule up and give her one bundle of fodder and three nubbins. And the preachers talked and walked around filling the little house and puffing and blowing as they washed their faces and hands in the tin basin.

"That is sho' a blessed stew you got cooking there, sister," said the oldest of the brethren, "my nose done testify."

"Amen," said another one.

"That ain't no stew," said the third, "that be's a roast and in the prime."

"And you eat, drink, and be satisfy," said the big preacher, "for you has labored mightily this day in the service of the most high King. Do tell."

"Ain't it the truth!" said the first brother.

And in no time at all they plopped themselves down at the table watering at the mouth and their noses sniffing hungry in the air. And the big preacher seemed to be feeling good too, he being a hypocrite, for he only bragged on his wife before company. So he upped and said how smart she was and what a fine supper she'd fixed for 'em all. The other three preachers out-bragged him now and said she was a fine helpmeet and the big preacher was blessed in his wife according to what the Good Book said. And then they set to the table and Brother Zebedee, the littlest one but with the biggest voice, led in a short slobbery prayer. And all the time the little woman kept going about waiting on 'em slow and still-eyed like one of them dummies you see at the fair, and didn't say a word. The whole roast was soon laid out on a wide plank in the middle of the table, and collard leaves and chopped pickle and big pieces of cabbage hearts were piled all around it.

"Seemed like this sheep sort of swunk," said the big preacher, sharpening up his knife on his big palm, ready to carve into it. Oh, yes, he'd have to find fault one way or another.

"Yeah, it do seem a little smaller than what you been talking 'bout, brother," the one called Zebedee spoke up. He was crippled and bent with rheumatiz.

"How is that?" said the big preacher to the little woman, his voice beginning to mutter low down in his chest like threatening something. "Don't tell me you done gone and overcooked it!"

"Some sheeps is like that," said the second Brother Lish, out of his great knowledge.

"But they ain't no going against the smell," said Brother Zebedee, "And it's got the right smell, ain't it, sister?"

"Yeah, the smell do specify," declared Brother Purge, the middle-sized preacher.

"But having had some experiences with sheeps," said Brother Lish all judgelike, "that head do look mighty sharp."

"Yeah," the little wife now said, "that's the way a sheep's head is—sharp and p'inted."

"But that's the most p'intedest head I ever did see," said Purge.

"But we'd ought to be thankful," Zebedee called out, "for what it likes in size it sho' is for a fact going to make up in quality of it, I can tell."

"Amen!" shouted the big preacher, striking the table with the butt of his hand. And so he begun working on the roast with his knife, serving it up to the preachers, and they all nodded and smiled and fell to eating hale and hearty.

Yes sir, it was a good sheep, the best they'd ever tasted, they kept declaring. But the woman didn't eat nothing. Said she weren't hungry. She sat scrooched up in front of the fire, and every now and then making a sucking sound with her teeth.

"Don't notice her," said the big preacher, "it's them risings in her jaw. She has 'em that-a-way."

During this time the two little boys had come back from putting up the Madge mule and were hanging around in the corner of the room looking on, 'cause among such great preachers all the children have to wait and eat last. And they mustn't say much, hardly a word. So these preachers smacked their lips and bragged on the rations till the oldest little boy, Silas, felt like he couldn't stand it no more, his tongue was plumb hasseling with hunger. He and little Paul had been so busy getting up the wood and working to help cook the roast all day that they had hardly had time to get a bit of rations for themselves, and their little stomachs were empty as dried gourds, with the seeds rattling in them. And soon it looked like there weren't going to be any sheep left for him or brother Paul. So he got over close to his mammy and whispered couldn't he have just a little teeny crumb.

"What's that boy talking about?" said the big preacher, looking out of his eye, red as that terrapin's. Little Silas dried up like a wet wisp of breath in the sun and the little woman didn't say nothing either.

"Them chillun's hungry," said Brother Zebedee, whose old toothless gums had begun to weaken on the roast, after he'd made away with several pieces whole.

"Yeah, give 'em something, brother," said Purge to the big preacher.

"That's right," Lish joined in, "for the Moster say share with one another even to the least smallest of His kingdom."

And so the big preacher, the daddy, called Silas over and said he mought have the head bone, for they'd already about cleaned it off. "You can use on that for the meanwhile time." You know how Negro preachers try to talk proper among themselves and out in company—"for the meanwhile time," he said.

Silas took the head bone and went over to the fireplace where little Paul was. And little Paul wrinkled his nose and suddenly said, "I bet Frizzle would like some of this, wouldn't she?"

"She would that," said Silas.

"And where is Frizzle?" said little Paul.

And the little woman kept her head bent over in her lap rocking her shoulders and sucking her teeth, and all the while little moaning sounds kept coming out of her throat with the pain of her risings.

"That's right," said Silas, "I ain't seen Frizzle all day."

They had been so busy helping their mammy cook the sheep they hadn't once thought of their dog. They slipped through the door and out into the yard, little Silas still carrying the head bone in his hand. And they began to whistle, and Paul called toward the creek, "Here, Frizzle, here Frizzle, come up here, Frizzle!" But Frizzle didn't come. And they whistled and called again, "Here, Frizzle, here, Frizzle, come up git somep'n t'eat!" But still no dog.

"You boys be quiet out there, where's yo' raising!" the big preacher roared. And the little fellows went on around the house and whistled and called softlike again. And all the time the preachers were eating away and talking about the big meeting now and the souls they had saved that day and how the devil had been run clean down into the Averysboro country and over beyond the river where folks was already cutting and killing each other no doubt in fighting scrapes. And they would have to move over there and carry on the battle. They were finishing up the sheep now and feeling full and holy.

"Yes," said the big preacher, pushing himself back from the table, "we have struck thunder-whacking blows in the vineyard of the Moster this day."

"Amen, do pray," said the other preachers.

"And the Lord has seen fit to bless us with a plentiful table as a sign of His grace and good will upon our good works and humble services."

"Amen," said Zebedee, "as was writ in Revelations, and John saw it all."

And all the while the poor little wife sat there in her chair scrooged up like a sick thrush.

"There's something here left," said her husband to her. "You'd better eat. Hear what I said?"

"I ain't hungry," she kept saying.

"How come you ain't hungry?" the big preacher wanted to know.

"Just ain't," she mumbled.

"Well, I reckon that's all right," said the big black man sorter snappy like, "'cause there ain't more'n enough left for both the two boys and a few gnawings for the dog."

And then the little boys came back in the room half crying and said, "Mammy, have you seen Frizzle?" And she begun to shiver and shake again. And putting her clean apron up to her face, she went over, threw wood on the fire, and sat down on the other side of the fireplace.

And the husband said, "Don't notice her. Ain't nothing ails her, just that little bit of toothache or pain in her head. I done said. She's the worst putonner they is with company round."

And then little Paul come whimpering up to her again and begging, "Have you seen Frizzle? I'm afraid she's lost or the gypsies have stoled her." In them days gypsies used to wander through the Little Bethel countryside camping here and there and robbing people's pigpens or chicken yards, so they said, though I've never known of an actual case. And sometimes they'd carry off babies, 'twas told.

Well, the poor little woman kept shaking her head and making a sort of moaning sound in her throat, and every once in a while she'd spit in the fire like her mouth was drooling from the pain of her aching teeth. The fresh dry wood broke into a wide blaze lighting up the room, and all of a sudden little Silas let out a great scream standing there in the firelight in the middle of the room and holding the head bone in his hand.

"Mammy, Mammy," he squealed.

"Hey, you!" yelled the black preacher. "Shut that fuss up!"

But this time little Silas didn't hush. And he began screaming louder and looking at the head bone which he held out before him, his eyes almost popping out of his face.

"What's the matter with that boy?" said Brother Purge lazily. "Is he having a fit?" Not that he cared, his belly being full of good rations now.

"Maybe some kind of power done struck him," said the second Brother Lish, "like the unknown tongues."

"I misdoubt he needs a praying off of spells," said Brother Zebedee eyeing him and pushing back his chair all ready to get down on his knees.

"Not a prayer but a beating for his misbehaving," the big daddy said. And he was about ready to jump in and destroy the little boy, when little Paul pointed his finger at the head bone and let out a scream too. "Looka there, looka there!" he yelled. The wood was burning bright in the fireplace now.

"I done told you, told you!" shouted the preacher again, drawing back his hands to slap 'em into kingdom come. But he didn't, for just then little Paul cried out, "That's Frizzle's nose.

That's the shape of it!" And he kept pointing his finger at the head bone.

"What's that? What's that?" said the daddy big preacher, and all the other preachers still holding their knives and forks in their hands looked up with their mouths wide open.

"Mammy done gone and cooked our dog!" little Silas screamed now, and he kept shaking and shivering and looking at the head bone in his hand.

"She's done killed Frizzle and cooked her!" little Paul wailed. Then the big preacher sprung out of his chair like a spasm had hit him and run to the door.

"Here, Frizzle!" he called. And all the other preachers pushed in a hurry back from the table and run to the door.

"Come up here, Frizzle, come up here, you dog!" they hollered.

And little Silas laid the head bone down on the table, and he and little Paul flew into the shed room and closed the door. And they could be heard weeping and wailing in there.

"Frizzle, I has called you before and you ain't come, but this time I wants you really to come!" said the big preacher. But no Frizzle.

All the while the poor woman sat there by the fire wagging her shoulders and wiping her eyes with her apron. The four preachers now run out into the yard calling, "Come up, Frizzle, come up!" Then they chased on around behind the house calling the dog, but still no answer.

Now in a minute what should be heard but the baa-baa of a sheep at the open door. And there looking into the room lighted by the firelight was the same old sheep, its head hung down and its eyes sad like an old man's, from the gash in its throat and the pain. It had come home again to Mammy to be fed no doubt.

And the little woman stood up, looked about her and then run out through the door and fell on her knees by the sheep and hugged it to her, crying like her poor heart would break.

And the preachers behind the house heard the baa-ing of the sheep, and they didn't have to call to Frizzle to come up any more.

For Frizzle came up now, and in a way you might think.

That's the end of the story, though it might be said that the big preacher, as soon as he had finished behind the house, did jump on his wife and tried to beat her to death, but the three preachers pulled him off and beat him instead. And 'twas said little Zebedee got a-straddle of him and nearly destroyed his face with his long razor-cutting claws. And from that day on he was a ruined man, so the story went. It was told how he left Little Bethel after that and was gone forever. And some time later the poor woman and the little boys left too. It was said he had sent for 'em from 'way off yonder. Why they wanted to go to him is a mystery to me. Maybe they were afraid not to go. And it was said before they left, the little boys buried Frizzle's bones in the backyard and put a headboard at the grave with some maypop blooms on it and some words burned on the plank saying how Frizzle sleeps here.

And the butterweeds and the mullein stalks grew up all around the house, and the doors rotted to pieces and fell in. And finally the devil in the shape of a big black dog with a face like that preacher's got to living in that house, so 'twas said, and at night would go out through the neighborhood stirring up trouble and raising a ruckus. And the people round and about went back to the ways of evil. There was cutting and killing and plenty of murder done in this neighborhood. So that's the way it was.

And the ruins of that house you can see there in the field near Cedar Grove Church to this day.

Jesus and the Wizzem-oose

~~~~~~

*H*e sat on the little snow-white cot in his iron cell, naked save
for a pair of white shorts which the male nurse had put on
him a few minutes before. He sat there bent over, his close-
cropped head gripped tightly in his big long-fingered black
hands and his bare feet resting on the cold cement floor. He was
tired. A sickish sort of sweet sleepiness kept smothering and
enveloping him, pulling him down in a nerveless lassitude. He
finally leaned back, toppled along the cot and lay there on his
side, his eyes closed.

He was walking down a long asphalt highway. On either
side the cold brown fields of dead cotton and cornstalks stretched
wide and faraway. He was moving swiftly along and with in-
credible ease. He came upon a group of dark-dressed white men
working by the road. They were digging a drain ditch with
enormously long-handled shovels. He then realized he had a
long-handled shovel in his hand too and was using it like a
vaulting pole the way he'd seen the students do at the University
and thus was moving with great leapings along the road. As
he sailed past the group of men they lifted their shovels and
wiggled them in greeting, giving a loud shrill hail of "Hi!"

"Hi," he answered back.

"Where ye bound for, Rudolph?" they queried all as one.

"On down the road," he shouted back, "I's seeking for to
find my Jesus!"

"Amen, amen!" they intoned in unison, waving their shovels at him.

He passed a house set with white pickets. Through the windows of this house he could see a strange uncouth and huge assortment of theatrical masks, costumes, shepherd's crooks, and other equipment like the stuff he'd seen them using once in a play at the University in Memorial Hall when he worked as a janitor there—except these were larger, more frightful, and terrifying.

And out of the depths of the house came a voice, half-hidden and smothered as it was amidst the huge medley of theatrical equipment, the voice of a little white girl calling plaintively to him—"Boy-ee! Boy-ee!"

This little girl was Eleanor Carrington, daughter of Professor Carrington up at the University. He had worked for the professor some in days gone by. When he was a boy years ago he and his father had hauled wood for him. He knew the little girl then. And though she didn't say so he knew she wanted him to come and help get her doll baby out of the well where it had fallen. But he couldn't stop. He had to keep moving, keep leaping with his shovel.

The sound of the little girl's voice with its piteous appeal had set up a dreadful stifling ache in his bosom. It was the old ache, the ache he had known for so many days and nights— of some dreadful happening to come. "Lawd ha' mercy on me!" he moaned.

He passed another house, somewhat similar to the front one but bigger and set likewise with white palings.

And hanging over the fence with a stern and iron aristocratic face was Dr. Carrington's once beautiful wife Alice, the mother of little Eleanor. And her gorgeous red hair was a fluffy autumn cloud down on her shoulders. Her beauty now was the beauty of death. Her cheeks were high and white-painted and her eyes darkened with the shadow of the fungus of death. She smiled at him as he leapt by, and her beauty was marred by several bad teeth.

But the smile took the ache out of his breast. In the lightened feeling he knew again what he wanted to know. He bleated out as he vaulted past, "Please ma'am, show me the way to find my Jesus."

The woman smiled again and nodded her head like a heavy-plumed dew-draggled flower.

"Through the wizzem-oose," she said.

And a little burst of shrill giggles came through her lips. She bowed her head waggingly about and rested her fine white throat on the point of one of the palings. Her feet were jumping up and down and her shoulders shaking with joy, but her iron face gazed out at him unblinkingly, and her white throat rested motionless on the point of the paling.

"Through the wizzem-oose," she repeated.

He went onwad now in great vaulting leaps like a kangaroo. There ahead of him was a wide stretching river with a bridge across it. The river was white like milk he saw spilling from a truck once and had a frosty sparkle on its surface in the sunshine. He sprang across the bridge and went up the incline of the hill beyond. In front of him there the road came to an end.

He looked about him. There was no river now nor any bridge, but everywhere as far as the eye could see and reaching up smotheringly about his shoulders and his face and mouth was a great frondy and feathery forest of red fern plants. This was the wizzem-oose, said the fear that chilled him through.

"Oh, oh, oh!" he whimpered in agony.

He looked to the east, to the south, to the west, and to the north. He whirled about and stood still. He stared ahead of him. And there showing clearly and almost like a twisting white worm through the wizzem-oose was a little pebbly path.

"I sees the true path!" he suddenly shouted.

His long-handled shovel was in the way now. He flung it from him and it fell far out in the ferny thicket. And as it fell, it made a clanging noise against the earth and lightning cracked and thunder reverberated across the sky.

He plunged up the little path and began fighting his way through the smothery ferns. And then with the medley and babblings of a multitudinous flock of clamorous and squeaking birds there came out of the ferns a bedlam of shrill voices.

And among the voices he could hear little Douglass and Mary Althy calling plaintively to him—his own two little children who had been burned to death in a fire in their old tenant shack close by the University one winter.

"Doody, Doody," they called, "Doody."

With great riving and gulping sobs he answered back, "Doody's coming, chillern, Doody's coming!"

And he floundered helplessly about trying to find them. Now he thinks he hears them just over there. He rushes there. Then he hears their voices behind him. He turns and rushes back. They're now here and now there, like the wandering rainy voices of spring frogs in the marshes.

He heard them calling under his feet. He dropped on his knees and began grabbling in the earth like a wild and maddened dog. And he kept yelling, "I's coming, chillern, I's coming to save you! Here's Doody, here he is!"

Suddenly he felt the earth heaving under him. He staggered to his feet. Coming across the great stretch of red ferns he heard the giant tread of a man. Then there was a second rocking of the earth and a second giant tread. He shrank down into the ferns. That was the law coming after him. He knew it too well. He stretched himself out flat behind a drooping fern, and peeping forth now he saw two tall figures, tall, tall, they were. And the wizzem-oose only came up to their knees. The ferns couldn't reach high enough to choke them. And they were wearing leather boots, the men were, and were dressed in rusty khaki, carrying riding crops in their hands like the girls at the riding academy, and automatic pistols at their belts. And as they went with monstrous walking steps onward, they beat about them in the ferns with their crops.

"He's bound to be in here," said the High Sheriff in a throaty rumbling voice. And the star of authority on his shirt front shivered and sparkled and glowed.

"He's good as dead then," said the deputy. And he threw his crop from him far toward the western horizon.

"Dead in the wizzem-oose," said the High Sheriff, and he likewise heaved his crop from him across the sky.

Then as if tickled at some vast and secret joke the two of them broke into ear-shattering laughter and hurried away, disappearing swiftly over the eastern horizon and into the oncoming gloom of night.

He lay there behind the droopy fern bush, his heart lifting within him. He was free at last. He was lost no more. He felt like singing. He stood up. Night had rolled in now. He set off walking swiftly along the little path.

"But where's my Jesus?" he said to himself. And his heart ached again.

He came to a little ravine with the waters of a spring rushing down it. He fell on his all-fours and drank his gullet full and stared at the little pool of water when it quieted beneath him. He could see himself reflected there in the suffused and glistening starlight—his gaunt cheeks and hollow eyes, his close-cropped head, all showing clear, and his great muscled shoulders glistening black and naked.

He heard a laugh behind him. And there sitting on a boulder was the penitentiary warden. He had a sparkling toy in his hand. It was a little electric chair that glowed with the radiance of a Christmas tree. Rudolph sat on his haunches and leaned back against the hillside.

"Well," said the warden. He was a squabby kindly-faced man. "What do you think of it?" and he jiggled the illumined electric chair up and down in the air.

"It's purty," the Negro gasped.

"You want it, huh?"

"Yessuh, give it to me, please suh," he gurgled. And he reached out his hand eagerly.

"I'll be giving it to you," said the warden. He put the shining chair into his pocket, hiding it away. "You're trying to find your Jesus, eh?" He cocked his head to one side and smiled.

"Yessuh," Rudolph said humbly.

"Well, look up. He's standing there in front of you."

Rudolph looked up, and before him stood the gentle figure of Jesus, his face sweet and smiling, his long hair parted back from his smooth forehead and his hand uplifted. His woman's tow-bagging dress hung straight and foldless down around him.

"Jesus, Jesus!" Rudolph shrieked deliriously. Plunging forward he fell in front of his Saviour and grasped his pierced feet and laid his cheek against them. And they were cold, even like the rock that he had laid his face on for a pillow when he was hiding away from the officers of the law that time in the deep Cape Fear River thicket.

"My son," said Jesus tenderly.

"My Saviour, my blessed everlasting and 'bundant Saviour," Rudolph babbled and sobbed.

"Now ain't that a purty sight of love and affection," said the warden.

The great sprawled form of the Negro lay there, ruined and spraddle-legged it lay, as he soaked in the sweetness of his salvation.

"Rest," said Jesus.

"Thanky suh, thanky suh," whispered Rudolph.

"He's a good man," said Jesus, glancing at the warden with his tender great eyes.

"Ho now," said the warden. "I know what you're going to say—like some them welfare folks up there at the University—that I do wrong in killing him!"

"Yes," said Jesus.

"Yes suh, yes suh," whimpered Rudolph in a pitiful small voice. "You does me wrong."

"Evil must pay for evil," said the warden harshly.

"But he's not bad any more," said Jesus. "His hard heart has been melted down."

"That's right, he confesses his sins," said the warden, wagging his head. "And he's getting right with God. They all do, they all get ready to go—loony with religion." And he smiled.

"He's now converted," said Jesus.

"Sure, sure," said the warden, "found you, Jesus."

"See, here he lies, filled with strength and love and glory—clinging close to his Saviour," murmured Jesus, looking sorrowfully down at the recumbent figure.

"That's good, that's good," said the warden, "let him cling, and he'll go away easy." He looked up at the sky. "It's getting on about ten o'clock."

"He's repented of the accident," said Jesus.

"I didn't mean to kill that landlord boss, suh, I, I just—I didn't mean to," moaned Rudolph there where he lay with his lips pressing the pitiful feet of his Lord.

"Too bad they proved you meant it," said the warden. "Sin has got to pay for sin."

"He's not a sinner now," said Jesus.

"That's what we've got this little chair for here in my pocket," said the warden, "to make 'em change—to help 'em find their Jesus."

"He's changed in the soul," said the Saviour.

"Yeh, in the soul. That's what religion does for you—and this little chair." And the warden patted his pocket.

"And the soul is what counts," said Jesus, still looking down at Rudolph.

"That's so—that's what counts."

"And seeing he's a good man now, Warden—then why do you want to kill him?"

"Hah, hah, hah," laughed the warden, wiggling his head.

"You say sin ought to pay for sin. That's better than saying that goodness must pay for sin." His voice was earnest now, a student querying. "Do you think so?"

The warden chuckled. "Now Jesus, you're trying to mix me up."

"I'm trying to understand—just trying to understand," the Saviour answered meekly, "And I in you and you in me—and both seeking for the truth." He went on. "Should we not let all good men live—especially so these days? The world needs its good men, I've heard tell. Looking about me, I would venture it does."

The warden smiled at him and winked. "There you go again," he said. "And the first thing you know, I misdoubt not you'll off and speak a parable. They make purty little stories, but the world don't live by 'em, them parables, no siree."

Rudolph suddenly chuckled where he lay. The warden looked over at him.

"Funny time for him to be laughing. Out of his great salvation he laughs."

"I been redeemed, suh, been redeemed," said Rudolph, still lying with his face against the feet of Jesus as before. And he crooned out a little stave of song—"Blessed be the sinners that have been redeemed."

"He sees the truth now," said Jesus compassionately. And he stretched out his hand and made a sign of blessedness over Rudolph.

"And what's that?" asked the warden with a hard smile. "The truth?"

Rudolph stirred on the ground, "Tell him, Jesus," he murmured, "tell him for po' me."

"He sees that it is yourself you kill, Warden. Every time you pull that switch you commit murder—murder on yourself."

"Well, well, who would have thought it?" said the warden. "It sounds like suicide—double multiplied. Ho, ho, I made a rhyme," he crowed.

Jesus turned and looked at him. "It shows in your eyes, Warden. Death shows in your eyes. Rudolph only dies once. Those more than a hundred men only died once. But you keep dying every time you kill a man. It enters into you—and it enters into me." He sighed and looked down again at the Negro. "The killed one grows used to death, the killer never does—except his own. There where the great killing was—in the east," and he gestured behind him, "is the deed fixed to eternity. They that were killed shall live forever in the event. And they who killed shall die daily and forever in their killing." The warden stared at him. "You are lost in the wizzem-oose, Warden," he said sadly.

Rudolph suddenly turned over, rolled away from Jesus, and beat the earth with thumping happy fists.

"Here now, here," said the warden angrily, and he pulled the little electric chair threateningly from his pocket. He looked up at the sky and put it back. "Not quite time," he said.

"I'm sorry, Warden, sorry," said Jesus. He raised his gentle brown hand and with the back of it wiped the sprouting tears from his eyes. The warden bent his head over, looking at the ground, saying nothing, waiting. Jesus looked around at Rudolph who lay stretched out, his face on his arm. "You've got a long trip," he said. "Rest now."

"Jesus, Jesus," murmured Rudolph. "Yes."

"Yes," said Jesus, "save thy soul." And he turned away and slowly disappeared into the wizzem-oose.

Rudolph felt him going. "Today I'll be with him in Paradise," he whispered to himself. A sense of sweet restfulness like the spilling of delicious sunshine crept over him and through him.

"And what do you want done with the body—send it to the University?" the warden queried suddenly.

"And that'll be all right too," said Rudolph. "Thankee, suh."

He felt himself sinking deep and deeper down into a feathery luscious darkness—deeper and deeper into the darkness which was inside himself. And that which was sinking was his own soul, his flame of life, the self itself. He knew it so. It was like a tiny illuminated moth that floated downward and ever downward into the endless dark.

What is the little moth after? Why does it float downward? Is there a current of air it rides out and over, ready to leap into the bottomless abyss? What is it doing, what is it seeking?

And look how it shines as it sinks, sinks. Its glowing little body now grows fainter and fainter to a tiny iota of light, no bigger than a pinpoint.

At the instant Rudolph saw it was about to fade to nothingness, he felt himself rushing wildly into the darkness after this little spark—hoping to cup it in his hands, to cherish it, to keep it from going out, even to warm it in his own bosom.

For he knew now it was his own soul, his life, his heartbeat, and he knew too the meaning of death.

"Save thy soul."

And in knowing the nature of death, he knew where he was as he rushed downward to save this spark of life. He knew that he was in a deep dark vertical shaft, and the opening of the shaft was above and behind him. And he could feel the light of the wide-awake day there. And his awareness was of the opening as his own mouth, and the shaft or tunnel down which he fled in pursuit of the little flame-tipped spirit not yet gone out into nothingness was his own gut.

And as he fled pursuingly he heard echoes and murmurs of wild and blasphemous beings, done to death, coming up from the interminable darkness waiting below there—the inky blackness in which this bit of flaming soul-stuff would be extinguished forever.

And onward, ever onward he plunged. And the vertical tunnel now became a turned and twisted horizontal one as he skeeted around the curves, rushing onward after the volatile little spirit.

The little spark suddenly disappeared ahead of him into the darkness. Death!

Rudolph woke with a shriek and sat up on his iron cot. The warden was there and the deputy, and behind them in the open cell door was the preacher with his Bible.

"We're ready, son," said the warden.

"Jesus, my Jesus," moaned Rudolph.

Then he heard in the air behind him, around him, the gentle inobdurate voice that speaks from everlasting to everlasting. "Fear not, I am with thee to the end," it said.

"Thankee, suh, thankee, suh," Rudolph gasped. And he straightened up, the misery slowly passing from his face.

"He's going cuckoo," said the deputy, "better hurry."

"They all do one way or another," said the warden.

They helped him to his feet. He stood there a moment, his whole form trembling like a fern plant in his dream—in the wizzem-oose. Then he began moving ahead, hurrying along out of the cell.

And the preacher followed slowly, intoning as he went. "Yea, though I walk through the valley of the shadow of death, I will fear no evil, for thou art with me—"

Supper for the Dead

The sun had gone down over the Oxendine clearing, and a sort of steaming night-sweat was creeping up and around the cabin from the feverish surrounding swamps. Fess Oxendine, a powerful Croatan Negro of middle age with a swarthy copperish face, stood by the pigpen holding a bucket in his hand and watching his pig eat slops. The raw-bony pig finished his guzzlings and squealed and gnawed at the rails for more, but Fess paid no attention to him now, as he stared on before him with unseeing eyes. The dusk gradually thickened in the little field, swamp owls began their mournful calling, and presently a mockingbird burst into a lonely chatter in the one peach tree near the garden. Fess with a mutter shook his shoulders and looked morosely around the sky. The spectacle of the west burning in a flame and the clouds marching in glory seemed to irritate and awe him. With a low oath, he lurched across his few potato rows and into the house. Sitting down by the fireplace, he began to dip snuff, now and then running his hand restlessly through his mop of heavy black hair.

"Why don't she come on here?" he grumbled. "And them owls, them owls, seem like they worse than used to." He slapped himself and muttered, "And them domn mosquitoes seem like they try to eat you up." He began beating about him with his ragged felt hat, and then he sat listening a moment. Finally, he lit a sputtering lamp, set it on the rough eating table and resumed his seat before the hearth. Then presently he lifted the lid from the spider sitting in the coals. "Hunh, left me nary a bite to eat. Knowed it. Mind to take my cowhide strop when she come and beat the clothes off'n her. Where she gone nohow?'' And he pondered that question for a while. "Something in her mind, that's a fact."

He wandered to the door, looked out, and gave a sharp whistle. As he waited with no reply, his face grew distorted with anger, and he yelled, "Heigh, you Vonie! Come out'n that 'ere swamp if you's down there!''

His old thin-flanked hound shook himself in the yard and coming up into the door leaned against his leg. The brute's gesture of kindliness infuriated Fess and with a savage kick he hurled the dog from him. In a burst of anger he sprang across the room, jerked down the gun from the wall pegs, and hurried to the door.

"Going to shoot that god-domn dog. Get from here, you dirty suck-egg devil! Always in the way." He raised his gun and fired, and the dog ran screaming across the field. He fired a second time and stood listening to the cries of pain dying toward the swamp. Then, heaving a great sigh, he set the stock of the gun on his foot. "Unh-hunh, I been telling that Nick to keep out'n my way. Anh, that purty sudden though, shooting him like that." He chuckled. "Sure tore up his tail with them bird shot, I betcha."

He stood thinking a while. "Seem like everything getting wrong with me lately. My head just flies slam to pieces. Wish I could forget that 'ere dream I had—oh—Lawd!" He groaned, shaking himself. "Next thing I'll be putting a load of shot into that Vonie."

He got two shells from the cupboard, reloaded the gun, and replaced it on the pegs above the door—after which he set about stirring up the fire and preparing supper. He placed a frying pan on the coals and began hacking off huge slices of white side meat at the cupboard.

Vonie shuffled quietly in. She was a middle-aged Negro, dressed in dirty rags, all hips and feet and with a polelike chest. One eye was missing from her head, leaving a red membranous slit between her lids. Her face was dead and sagging and unrelieved by any vitality, even in her one good eye, and her complexion was creamy and unbelievably delicate like the inner petal of a magnolia bloom.

As she entered, Fess whirled upon her with a shout, raising the knife in his hand. "Yeah, and where you been to, 'oman!"

Vonie dragged off her bonnet and sat quietly in a chair. "Off," she replied.

"Reckon I knows it, and you gone the whole evening," growled Fess. He grabbed her shoulder and put the knife against her throat. "Gooder mind to rip your gullet open. Where you been to, I axes you?"

"Off," Vonie choked, "off a little piece."

He crushed her down in her seat. "Spit out!" he demanded. "What you up to?" She closed her eye and dropped her head limply against his hand. "All right, I'll find out," he threatened, giving her throat a little sharp prick. "Better not be up to no tricks," he chuckled as he stepped back from her. "You know me."

With her apron she wiped a tiny ooze of blood from her throat where the knife had nicked her, and spoke in a thin stifled voice. "Gouge t'other eye out, anh?"

Fess threw his knife down and slumped into a chair. "Man's 'oman tell the sheriff on him ought to have 'em both bored out with a chunk of fire."

"Ain't no sheriff this time."

"Better not be." Then eyeing her, he added, "But you act so quare all day long! Something in your mind?"

"They is," she said quietly.

Fess punched up the fire and spoke softly without looking around, "Still worrying about it—about something?"

"Mought."

"Quit it, quit it. Can't be helped."

"Mought could a month ago," she said sharply. Then she bowed her head in her hands. "Poor little thing!" she whispered.

"Hanh?"

"Poor little thing."

"Here now," he reproved sharply, "thought you done say all mebbe for the best."

"Mebbe—" She paused and then went on levelly as she

darted a quick look at Fess, "I been turning it in my head." She stared at the floor.

"Then what you been doing off in them woods?"

"Never mind."

"Don't talk too sharp with me, nigger."

She suddenly broke into a low sardonic and toothless laugh. Fess turned and gazed at her in astonishment, then shrugged his shoulders. "Your misery make you laugh like that," he said carelessly.

"Mebbe."

"By God," he exploded, bounding out of his chair, "you stop that and get busy about my supper." He moved toward her. "Here I been waiting, and I got to hurry to the swamps."

"Better not go to that whiskey still tonight, Fess."

"Hunh?"

"I hearn the deputies is on to it. They watch tonight," Vonie continued in the same impersonal voice.

"That's the truth?"

"Mebbe."

"Here—" He stopped uncertainly. "Quare you telling me that. Seem like you'd want 'em to get me, way they done t'other time, and I served two years in the pen."

"Don't want 'em to get you this time," she said.

"Not if you wants to keep that head where it belongs," he muttered. With a touch of kindness he asked, "Where you hear about them officers, Vonie?"

"Over the creek."

"What you doing over there?"

"A little business."

"A little business!" he raged. "Cut out that making fun of me." Then with a sudden thought he queried uncertainly, "You ain't tell them officers they find me here, has you?"

"I ain't told 'em nothing."

"Can't see what you planning," he puzzled.

Vonie gave him another quick glance. "Lonesome here by myself now," she stated. "Be bad with you in the penitenshur again."

"Sure then," said Fess, gruffly, "but I be here with you now."

"Mebbe."

He stared at her in angry amazement. "What in the name of God you mean, 'oman, with all that mebbe talk?"

She smiled queerly and sweetly at him. "How long since it happened?" she asked.

"Don't put no 'membrance upon it. Forget it, let it go by."

"About a month, ain't it, since us found her in the water?"

"Well then, about a month!"

"New-moon night?"

"Don't know," said Fess. "Can't 'member all that," he hurried on. "Quit fetching it up, I tell you." In a decisive voice, he quoted, " 'She up above now, at rest.' Precher say she a good girl."

"Her was good," Vonie affirmed with sudden vehemence. "But then somebody was mean."

"How come?" Fess asked softly—a little tentatively and softly.

"Who put her in that creek and drownded her?"

"Done told you she musta slipped in when she was fishing."

"Why ain't you tried to find out who 'twas?" she demanded passionately. "You her daddy?"

"She got drownded, that's all."

"Fess Oxendine," she cried out in a sudden burst of excitement, "who done it, who was the man?"

"How the hell I know!" he snapped at her. He went over to the bed and lay down. "I gwine lie and snooze a minute," he announced. "Get on now and fry me that meat."

Vonie began to beat on her knees. "Some of 'em say she drownded herself and gone down to hell," she burst out frantically, "they say it that day at the graveyard."

"She fell in, I tell you, and got that fishline all wropped around her neck. That choked her down."

Vonie stood up accusingly. "And what you doing last night talking about fishlines in your dreams?" she insisted. Then as she watched Fess and saw him start, she added, "And one time you hollered out and called, 'O purty flower!' "

He answered after a moment, cunningly, "Et too much of that grease and side meat, make me have bad dreams. Quit worrying. She gone up to heaven. Sure she sorry for you and me way down here."

"I'm going to find out where she gone," Vonie announced mournfully.

"Hunh?"

"Find out."

"You must be crazy in the head or something," he snorted. "How you going to do that?"

"Find out who done it too," she threatened.

"How you mean?" Fess sat up on the edge of the bed.

"Help coming here. Us going to find out."

He spoke in a low voice, "Who coming?"

"I been over to Aunt Queenie's."

"That 'oman ain't coming to my house," Fess shouted, and he sprang up from the bed.

"Her and the twins is coming here in a few minutes."

"Them snake folks come in here," warned Fess, getting his gun, "I fill 'em full of lead."

"She don't care nothing for that."

"Where they now?"

"They come by the graveyard to get some dirt off'n her grave."

"I'll kill 'em, I tell you!"

Vonie sat down again and watched him intently. "Nunh—unh, you won't," she stated. "Lead won't bother 'em, and besides, they'd ha'nt you and destroy you with their power."

"Hunh, that ha'nt business!" he jeered. "What they going to do here?"

"They show you."

Fess set his gun down against the wall. "Pshaw," he shrugged, "they can't hurt me. Keep strong in the head, that's all. Mess with me and I get me a stick and frail 'em out'n here."

Vonie laughed toothlessly. "You the only man'd say that."

"And I's the man can do it, too." He threw up his head. "You lowdown niggers all got no more sense than a gang of sheep. Fess Oxendine ain't that sort. He's smart. He got the white folks' blood in him, and that old Indian chief was my grandpap. Yeh," he boasted "let 'em try all their mess, it won't scare me."

"Sure," she replied cryptically, "you too much man for the nigger trash."

"All that business about Jack-muh-lantern and that Plateye—hunh," he sneered, "I seed 'em and it weren't never nothing but old fox fire or lightning bugs." He laughed. "And you niggers all freezing with the fear of 'em!"

"Sure," said Vonie in a quiet voice, "that's all." She went to the chimney, took a little brown packet from a nail and threw it into the fire.

"Heigh!" shouted Fess, "what you doing?"

Vonie returned impassively to her chair. "Sure you don't care if I burn up my little conjure trick," she taunted. "They ain't no power in it, you said so many a time."

"You don't want to burn it up now with old Queenie coming here," he protested as he moved toward the fireplace.

"Queenie ain't going to hurt me." Fess stopped and Vonie laughed sarcastically, "No, he ain't skeered of nothing. He strong in the head and all-powerful!" she scoffed. Then in a monotone she went on, "Fess Oxendine, the mighty man of the Cumberland swamps, don't have to put no dependence in no conjure bag. He strong enough without it, the wild buck of the river. How many men has he cut to the hollow? And the women, and the women! Bad Fess they calls him." Then she pointed teasingly toward the fire—"Better not let that little bag burn up."

"Domn that little bag!" barked Fess. "What I care?" He turned and kicked at her. "Get now, and fix my supper!"

Vonie laughed softly. "We all eat supper together," she said.

"Hunh?"

"Supper for the dead."

"What's that?"

"Us going to feed her, poor little thing."

Fess stared at her in perplexity.

"That studying about it," he mumbled, "got her wrong in the head."

A clutch at the latch and old Queenie stood in the doorway. Fess looked at her a moment and then resumed his seat near the fire. The old woman came in, followed by her twin daughters, Lil and Fury. She was an incredibly ancient Guinea Negro of a bluish-black color, drawn and skinny, with bright little eyes, and dressed in a single garment of dull red flannel. She walked with the aid of two sticks and carried a little leather satchel on her arm. The twins, about sixty years old, and similarly dressed, followed her with their short quivering palsied steps, their tiny bonneted heads rising above their shoulders with the grace and litheness of two snakes. As they entered holding hands, they fastened their beady eyes on Fess who moved closer against the wall.

Queenie motioned with her stick. "Set over there, chillun," she directed in a husky, jerky voice.

The twins moved over and sat down on the edge of the bed. Old Queenie looked carefully around the room and smiled triumphantly as her eyes rested on the packet burning in the fire.

"Set down and rest yourself," said Vonie, rising and placing her a chair.

"Who that man?" asked Queenie huskily.

"That Fess, the daddy of her," Vonie said, pointing to her husband who sat watching them narrowly.

"Sure that Fess," Queenie smiled pleasantly. "Bad man, ain't you, Fess?"

Abstractedly pulling out his box of snuff, Fess growled out, "What you doing here in my house?" He turned his head away and began dipping up the brown powder with his twiggy brush. "Old 'oman what the snakes used to suck," he muttered.

A sudden gleam came into Queenie's eye, quickly passing away as she inquired politely, "How you all getting on?"

"Getting on all right up to now, and you might take them two bastards off my bed and hit the grit from here."

"Don't mind us, Fess," soothed Queenie. "There ain't no harm in us. Gimme a bit of your snuff, Fess," she begged, smiling kindly at him. The twins leaned forward expectantly.

"Sure I don't mind that. Help yourself," he said. She reached for the snuff and put some in her lip and nose as he watched her thoughtfully. "You don't seem so quare after all," he acknowledged, as Old Queenie suddenly sneezed and then inhaled with a deep breath of delight. "But," he added, "them two 'omans on that bed—oom—"

Queenie sneezed again and smiled at him. "Them poor harmless children. But ain't they purty, Fess? I calls 'em my two snakes. Talk to him, chillun."

They licked their tongues out at him.

Fess started back with an exclamation. "Great God, them things ain't human!"

Vonie sat quietly, saying nothing.

"Oh, they can talk better than that," squeaked old Queenie. "They can say words at times. Poor things, got marked by a big rattlesnake pilot bit me in the swamp before they was born." She sneezed again and the twins grew more and more excited, their heads appearing to rise higher and higher on the stems of their scrawny necks.

"Make 'em quit looking at me that-a-way," Fess ordered, as she handed the snuff box back to him.

"That mighty good snuff, Fess," purred the old woman. She sneezed twice in rapid succession and turned and looked at the twins. Their tongues began to flutter between their lips as they hungrily watched their mother.

"Why you sneeze so?" Fess asked suspiciously.

Vonie looked up intently.

With her gaze still fixed on the twins, Queenie spoke gently over her shoulder, "Good snuff, Fess, good 'Lord o' God.'" She opened her mouth, wrinkled her nose, and then sneezed sharply. The two on the bed sat up stiff and straight. Queenie shouted out, "Seven times, chillun, seven times!" She tottered to the door and looked out over her left shoulder. "There it is, there's the new moon behind that poplar. All ready, fixed and ready, fixed and ready."

"Don't you start that 'ere business, I tells you!" yelled Fess, rising out of his chair.

"Set down in that chair, nigger man," Queenie snapped with a sharp gesture. "Set down."

Fess gradually sank back into his chair, muttering, "But mind what I done told you."

He sat waiting.

Impressively the old woman raised her head and spoke into the air.

"God before me,
God behind me,
God be with me."

"God be with me," came in a sort of half-whisper from Lil and Fury where they sat on the bed.

"That right, talk out, speak forth, chillun," urged the old woman. "There was li'l Miny drownded in the creek. Where she now?"

Vonie bowed her head on her knees as the twins mumbled together, "Where?"

"Mebbe in heaven, mebbe in hell, mebbe walking in the swamps," shrilled Queenie. "Us going to find out, going to raise her ghost from the dead and feed her, going to see who killed her."

"Who kill her," echoed Lil and Fury vacuously.

"Reckon you won't be getting the dead back here," laughed Fess brutally—as he reached for his gun and laid it across his lap.

Queenie touched Vonie's bent back with her stick. "Fetch me her dress and bonnet." Vonie rose and brought them from a nail in the wall. And the old woman placed a chair to the table, spread the dress over it, and put the bonnet on top, forming a crude dummy. Fondling his gun, Fess watched every movement with skeptical braggadocio. Old Queenie called, "Chillun!"

Lil and Fury answered softly, "Yeh, ma'am."

"Can you hear me?"

"Us hear you."

"Can her hear me?"

"Her hear you too."

"Us got the power," chuckled Queenie.

"The power," reiterated Lil and Fury.

"Fetch me three plates and the bowl, 'oman."

Vonie went to the cupboard and brought the dishes to the table where old Queenie set them out, a plate before the dummy, one at each end of the table and the bowl in the middle.

"Such a pack o' fools!" scoffed Fess in a loud reassuring voice.

"Come to the table, chillun."

With jerky steps the twins moved from the bed and seated themselves, one at each end of the table. Queenie opened her satchel and took out a dirty little paper bag. She let the contents sift through her bony fingers into the bowl. "Pour in, pour in," she quavered, "dirt from her grave."

"The graveyard dirt," intoned the twins.

Old Queenie pulled out a handful of herbs and placed them in the bowl. "Bring me the fire-coal, 'oman," she commanded.

Vonie raked a fire-coal onto a chip of wood and brought it. Queenie's withered hand closed over the live coal and holding it close to her mouth she blew upon it.

"Great God," gasped Fess in astonishment, "her hand like iron. It don't burn her!"

She laid the glowing ember in the bowl. "Blow on it, chillun."

They bent their snakelike heads toward the center of the table and blew with a whistling sound. Presently a curl of smoke rose upward.

"Breathe that smoke down in you."

They inhaled the fumes and sat stiffly back in their chairs, looking unblinkingly at old Queenie who reached once more down into her satchel. She drew out several pieces of greasy white meat and placed one in each of the three plates. "Eat that, chillun," she whispered huskily.

They began to eat. Vonie came up near the table and stood looking on. Fess watched in horrified silence. Then he burst out, "What that they eating? I bet to Christ that rashers of dead folks!"

"See anything yet?" asked Queenie, leaning close to the twins.

"Not yet, mammy," they replied dreamily.

She pulled out three dark objects resembling frogs and

placed them on the plates. "Eat that, chillun." And she peered into their eyes as they continued to eat. "See yet?" she queried.

"Not yet, mammy."

"What that, chillun?" asked Queenie hoarsely.

"Something 'way, 'way in a big snow field."

Fess jumped out of his chair. "God Almighty," he screeched, "they eating frogs!"

Queenie waved her hand behind her, and Fess gradually sank back into his chair, staring at the three of them with open mouth.

"Look close, look close," and Queenie turned back to the twins who now sat motionless as if entranced. "Is there people there?"

"People there," they reassured her.

"Her there?"

"Can't see um."

Old Queenie pulled out more dried herbs and put them in the bowl. Thick clouds of smoke poured upward and settled about the room. "Breathe it, chillun," she urged, "breathe it." She took a little red flannel pouch out of the satchel and spilled some white powder on each of the three plates. The twins wet their bony fingers and dipped the powder into their mouths. "Look down," she coaxed them on, "way down yonder in that other place. Look down."

"Us looking," Lil and Fury spoke together in a faraway voice.

"Can see her?" insisted Queenie. They suddenly drew back horrified. "Look!" she screamed, "look there!"

"Ah!" they shuddered, closing their eyes and swaying hypnotically from side to side.

"Look down there. I tell you!" she slobbered eagerly. Reaching again into the satchel, she pulled out a handful of hair and cast it into the bowl. A sudden quick puff of flame went upward, and Lil and Fury reared back with a low moan.

Vonie dropped down whimpering in her chair. "Don't make 'em look, don't make 'em!" she shuddered. "They done seen something bad." She hid her face in her arms and rocked from side to side in grief.

"Look down there," commanded Queenie. "Look down."

"Can see now."

"See her?"

"Poor little Miny down there in hell!" wailed Vonie, covering her head with her apron.

With fierce concentration Queenie urged the twins on—"Keep your eye on her, don't lose her." She began to chant in her cracked voice as she drew fetishes from the satchel and arranged them on the table.

"Feathers, cakes and beans and corn,
Thumb of the bastard son just born.
Spider, wasp and field-mice tongue . . ."

Here Fess shot out of his chair, yelling, "I done see that 'ere bonnet move on the chair!" He jerked his gun up to the ready.

Queenie went on with her chant—

—*"Eye of a man the gallows hung."*

"You quit that conjure business! Don't, I shoot you!" snarled Fess. Holding his gun aimed at the three, he began to back toward the door, but Old Queenie stepped before him with her stick upraised.

"You ain't going out'n here, black man, till we's done." With a quick movement of her stick she bent down and drew a line on the floor from the door to the fireplace, enclosing Fess. "You step over that line," she threatened, "and you fall dead."

Fess put out his foot as if to step over the line, while Queenie watched him with her withered arm uplifted. The twins moaned loudly. Finally he turned and slunk back to his chair and sat down shiveringly. "All right—God domn—you! I—wait and see—see what you up to," he mouthed half to himself.

Queenie laid out more fetishes—

"Devil's snuff and the dried dog brains,
'Oman's scabs that died in chains.
Ground calf-tongue and the black cat's bone—"

She raised her voice in a high pleading.

"Come up, Miny, get your own!"

Weakly, Fess beat himself with his hat. "That domn smoke make me feel quare," he coughed huskily. "Hunh, I keep strong in the head, that's what. They can't hurt me. That old bonnet there limp as a rag yet."

From her chair Vonie whined under her apron, "Miny, Miny!"

"Where she now, chillun?" cackled Queenie.

"Can hardly see, about gone."

"Keep looking, keep looking!" She took out an egg and broke it into the bowl. Then she poured a small bottle of fluid in. She resumed her chant of incantation—

"Black snake ile and raincrow egg,
Put the strength in the ghostes leg.
Make 'em power of muscle and bone—
Come up, Miny, here's your own."

"Here's your own," chorused Lil and Fury.

"I see what you after now!" raged Fess. "You wants to ha'nt me. But you ain't going to do it. I'll blow your brains out with this here." He cocked his gun and leveled it at them. "I give you just one minute to get out!" he threatened fiercely.

Old Queenie paid no attention to him, her head lifted up as if straining toward a vision.

"Us see her now," cried the twins joyously. "Her coming."

"Coming!" exulted Queenie loudly.

"Here goes then," shouted Fess, "and that's the last of you. I shoot the old black 'un first."

As though he had not spoken, Lil and Fury went on. "Her in the field out there now," they announced joyously.

Queenie threw her hands up and down in the air. "Yes, yes," she sang out. "I feel it."

"I shoot both o' them eyes out!" yelled Fess, his face distorted with rage.

He pulled the trigger, but the hammer refused to fall. Frantically he tried the other one. "Them domned hammers stuck." He raised the gun again.

Old Queenie turned and looked at him with a low devilish laugh. "Come on, Miny, here's your own," she called.

"Here's your own," echoed Lil and Fury.

"She done got that gun—a spell on it!" shrieked Fess. He threw the gun from him and whirled to his chair. Sitting down with his back to the women, he clasped his head between his knees, rocking and moaning. "My head done all gone to pieces. O Lord, have mercy on me!" He cowered in his seat.

"Her in the yard out there now," declared the twins.

"Yes, yes," shrilled Queenie ecstatically, "fetch her in." She began to call loudly, "Supper, Miny! Come to your supper."

Suddenly Vonie threw her apron from around her head and sat up calm and straight. "Call her, call her, lemme see her onct more."

Queenie turned and looked through the door. "Look there, look there," she pointed. "Her out there at the well drawing water."

The low rumble of a whirring windlass was heard from the gloom outside.

Fess raised his head. "Listen at that, listen at that!" He crouched down on the hearth. "That's a ha'nt drawing water at my well," he whimpered as he sat shaking in terror.

"The ha'nts draw water at his well," echoed Lil and Fury.

"The yard's full of 'em, all come back with her," observed Queenie staring out in the deepening dusk. "Fess," she exulted, "you is a lost member." She reached out her shriveled arms toward the night and pleaded, "Come in here, Miny, come on in!" Then she turned to the twins, "Call to her, chillun," she urged breathlessly. "Call to her."

"Hear us, Miny, hear us!" begged Lil and Fury, beating their heads against the table in the intensity of their supplication. "Come in. The supper is waiting, the supper is fixed."

"Look! Look! She about to turn back. Feel for her, Vonie," gasped Queenie. "Her gwine back in the field with all them others, the little 'uns and the big 'uns. They gwine back to the swamps."

"Miny!" Vonie wailed loudly, "Miny, come to your poor muh this night!"

"Her coming, her coming in," Queenie raised a joyous cry. She addressed the specter beyond the door. "That's it, honey, that's it, come on in." Her voice trembled and slobbered with eagerness, and she began patting her hands softly together, keeping time with her foot on the floor.

"There she now!" Vonie screamed out.

She sat petrified in her chair. A ragged Negro girl with downcast eyes came quietly in at the door, seated herself at the table, and suddenly "inhabited" the clothes. She was about sixteen years old, with swelling breasts and a plump oval face. She began eating food from the plate.

Vonie murmured, "Miny, Miny, is that you, chile?" She stared at the apparition with fascinated eyes. "Then you ain't dead, thank God!" she gasped. "Fess," she cried, "there's Miny, come back to us!"

" 'Tain't nothing, 'tain't nothing," whimpered Fess. "Don't look at that."

Suddenly old Queenie began to caper back and forth across the floor, breaking out into senseless ecstatic words. "Tibbity-bibbity, tchee-tchee-tchee—Tchee-tchee-tchee. Purty little flower."

"Purty little flower," chanted Lil and Fury, falling on the floor now and making obeisance before the little girl.

Queenie waved her arms aloft. "Lily of the valley," she sang.

"Little scrushed lily!" Lil and Fury bowed their foreheads up and down.

"The rose o' Sharon," intoned Queenie.

"Rose o' Sharon," carolled the twins.

"Mean man pulled the little flower from its bed."

"Mean man pulled."

"He have to die."

"Got to die."

"Who were it, honey?" cried Queenie, peering intently at the girl who continued eating her food, saying nothing.

"Who were it?" Lil and Fury repeated.

Queenie cried out, "You, Fess Oxendine, look up here and see your daughter!"

"I can't," sobbed Fess, "can't see her. Have mercy on me!"

"Look up, I tell you."

Queenie stretched out her hand, and Fess slowly lifted his head. "Who that?" he gasped, joy breaking in his voice. "Why that—Glory to God, that little Miny come back!" He staggered to his feet and went toward the table. "Then you ain't dead, thank the Lord. That all a dream I had." He suddenly broke into loud heart-easing sobs. "Thank the Lord, thank the Lord!"

As he approached the table, the little girl backed away in terror and moved toward the door.

"Miny, Miny!" wailed Vonie.

"Tell us who the man?" demanded Queenie.

Without lifting her head, the little girl nodded at Fess.

"I knowed it!" cackled Queenie. "Fess the man what ruint you and made you drownd yourself." She reached into the bowl, and a galvanic shock seemed to run through her emaciated body. She threw bits of the bowl's contents toward the door and the little girl disappeared into the darkness. And the clothes were left on the chair again. Vonie started up, wailing, "Where she gone? Give her back to me, give her back!"

Queenie threw part of the mixture on Fess, "Here the man!" she squealed.

"Let me loose!" screamed Fess, clawing at the back of his neck. "Who that got me!"

He fell writhing and howling on the floor.

"There he, Vonie," Queenie declared, "he the man mix with his own flesh."

"Look at the bad man lying there cutting up on the floor," Vonie broke out, laughing loudly and hysterically. "That you, Fess, the old swamp buck?"

"Couldn't get her out'n my mind," he gasped, clawing his clothes from him. "Ooh—let me loose!"

Suddenly Vonie picked up the gun and fired both barrels into Fess's back. Then she flew out through the door calling pitifully after the little girl—"Miny! Miny—wait!"

"The power come down to us," called Queenie, her face illumined. She sprinkled Lil and Fury with the contents of the bowl, and they rose from the floor.

"The power," they sang out, raising their transfigured faces.

"Us reach and call and the dead do answer," exulted Queenie, skipping as she chanted.

"Do answer," the twins called, following her.

She wove a dancing pattern around Fess's dead body. "Hallelujah!" she shouted.

"Hallelujah!"

"Us call and get answer." The three figures began to clap their hands as the dance quickened, and they swayed and bowed and chanted.

"Us call and get answer."

"Get answer."

"The supper fotch 'em."

"Fotch 'em down," the twins laughed in ecstasy.

"Supper for the dead."

"For the dead."

The twins continued dancing around the body as Old Queenie went hopping about the table, raking her charms and fetishes into her bag. Their breath came through their teeth in a hissing sound.

Queenie danced toward the door. "Tibbity-bibbity-tchee-tchee-tchee," she gibbered.

"Tchee-tchee-tchee," hissed the twins. The three disappeared through the door, their outlandish vocables dying across the fields.

The Lost Ford

T*he big Dominicker rooster* stood up in the maple tree, flapped his wings, and crowed. His pale crafty eye had discerned the first gleam of coming dawn across the wide fields. A low ruffling and guggling stirred among the hens on the limbs around him. He crowed loudly again and flew down into the yard, the hens following him. The flock went scratching around the back door of the Negro cabin, with their wings tight against their bodies like buzzards walking, and out into the edge of the cornpatch where a few late peas were to be found.

Arth Loring and his wife Ada in their bed heard the crowing, and Arth got up, pulled on his trousers, and slid on his thick knitted socks as fast as he could.

"Lord, getting late. Day done 'bout broke," he said.

He stumbled toward the fireplace where his lightwood splinters and four little logs of oak wood were piled from the night before, struck a match, and built a fire. He'd have to get a move on, he would. Today was the day of his plans. Presently the fire was leaping up the chimney and he crouched before it rubbing his numb hands and warming his brogan shoes, stiff from the cold.

"What time is it now?" Ada called.

" 'Bout four o'clock," he answered. "I'll build you a fire in the stove."

"Oh, me my," she yawned, throwing the bedclothes from her. She raked up her garments lying in a bundle on the floor and came to the fire dressed in an old outing flannel wrapper. Unashamed, she dropped the wrapper to the floor about her feet, and nakedly shivering got into her underclothes and slid her dress over her head. Then she sat down by the fire and pulled on her stockings and shoes.

"Better put some tallow on your shoes, Arth," she said.

"Ain't got no time now—and whew, is it cold!"

When the fire was going in the stove, he went out and fed his mules. Ada cooked the breakfast. While the meat was frying and the bread baking, she returned to the room and went over to the bed where the three children were sleeping.

"Get up, son. Your pa's soon ready to go." She put her hand beneath little Bennie's head and lifted him up. The little fellow sat up blinking, his head nodding. She turned away to the kitchen again and he fell back on the bed, sound asleep.

When Arth had fed his two mules, he threw a few ears of corn to the three fattening hogs and went around into the backyard to examine his tobacco loaded on the wagon. He raised the frosty quilt covering and pushed his hand into the high pile of sweet-smelling leaves. They were flexible and smooth—as— well, smooth as Ada's sweet brown skin under her clothes, he suddenly thought.

"Sure in fine order," he chuckled. Ada leaned her head out of the door.

"Breakfast on the table!"

He tucked the quilts in around the tobacco and buttoned up his coat. It was cold all right, cold and frosty, and a little bitter wind was blowing from the northwest. He looked up at the stars to see how the weather was standing, and all was cold and clear as a bell. He went in and sat down by the table under the smoky lamp.

"Where's that Bennie, Ada?"

"Lord, I called him long ago." She hurried in and jerked the boy out of bed.

"Good gracious alive, look at him sleeping his head off, and his pappy gonna take him to the 'bacco sale." He trotted to the fire with his clothes and put them on. Arth and Ada began eating their breakfast of bread and bacon, coffee and grits. Bennie came in and took his seat on the bench.

"I ain't hongry, Muh." But she heaped his plate high with food.

"Lord," said Arth, "that trip done took away his appetite."

"Here, drink this. It'll help get the sleepy out'n them eyes and make you feel good." She put a cup of hot coffee before him. Bennie poured it out into his saucer, blew upon it to cool it, and drank it down, peering outward at his parents with big soft eyes.

"Don't that boy grow, Ada?"

"He do, same as a man, about."

"Look at him setting up here at the table, drinking his coffee. Next year I'll have me a plowhand sure enough."

"I plowed some this year," said Bennie quickly.

"That he did, round the old dunghill. Next year I'll put you in the newground with that jumping coulter."

"Yay, yay," said Bennie joyously.

"Don't rush him too fast, Arth," said Ada.

Arth got his old overcoat from a nail on the wall. He fastened it across his breast with a wooden peg and pulled on his old plug hat that had a hole in the top of it.

"I'll go catch the mules and put 'em to the wagon. Get him ready." For a moment he stood looking at his wife, winked at her, and then broke into a low happy chuckle.

"What ail your pa, sonny?" Ada asked. Little Bennie made no reply but eyed his father soberly. "What you keeping from me, Arth?"

" 'Bacco brought a big price yestiddy. Mr. Will Connelly got forty cents a pound for them two truck loads he sent up there. Sure good price."

"Was a good price," Ada echoed somewhat queryingly.

"I been a-figgering," and again he winked. "Reckon how much that thirteen hundred pounds bring us—and they must be that much according to my figgering—or more. They ain't no better 'bacco been made in this country. Mr. Hugh Morgan say so hisself. Mought bring me six-seven hundred dollars."

"We don't owe nothing neither."

"No, all done paid."

"Mought put a slam of money in the bank this time."

"Mought, and mought not."

"What you fixing to do, Arth?" And she gave him a bright, warm smile as in the old days when they first went together.

"You just wait. I come bringing you a surprise mebbe." He went up to her and gave her a kissing smack on the cheek. "You about the best gal I ever did see. Sure," he murmured softly.

"Shucks—oh, shucks. Go on." She turned away to hide the tears that rose in her eyes. She was foolish that way, soft-hearted, and always would be maybe, and she loved this man, she loved him so.

Arth went out, bridled and harnessed his mules, and hitched them to the wagon. The iron traces and breast chains were freezing cold, and at times he had to stick his fingers in his mouth to warm the aching sting and numbness out of them. Ada put a little coat with a piece of old sweater under it on Bennie, pulled his cap down tight on his head, and sent him out to his father. She got a brick which she had heated on the stove, took it out, and put it beneath the wagon seat.

"I declare I slam forgot that brick," said Arth. "You never forget nothing, do you, honey?"

"Wanter keep my boys warm."

When they had mounted to the seat, she helped tuck them in and stood watching them drive away. The wheels on the newly greased axle rolled softly over the iron-hard ground, and the mules blew white steamy breaths into the frozen air. Down the little lane they went and around the bend into the big road that led to the north toward the market town of Durham. Arth sat aloft on his seat and cracked his whip, twirling the seasoned hickory staff above his head. The sun was not up yet, but the east was red and fiery like a great burning woods. High up in the edge of the night gloom which was running away fast to the west, the morning star shone like a big flower. Arth put his arm around little Bennie and hugged him up close and warm.

"Cold, sonny?"

"Nary grain. What star is that, Pappy?"

"That's the morning star."

"What do it do?"

"It shines up there, up there in heaven."

"Heaven's where God is, ain't it?"

"Yeh, God's up there." They drove along silent.

"What do he do, Pappy?"

"Who?"

"God."

"He watch over everything."

"See everything?"

"See you and me and these two mules and this 'bacco. See your mammy back there at home working away."

"God won't hurt you and me, will he, Pappy?"

"Lord, listen at him! That he won't—that's a good God. He take care of you and me and Mammy and little Sis and Babe Teensy."

"Do God make the star shine and make that sun come up?"

"God do everything. He a much man. Lord, he strong. The muscles on his arm big as them bee gums back of the house. When he lifts up his arm, the muscle swell out same as old Broadhuss. See them hills there where the sun's rising? God pile 'em up with his hands. See them low-grounds there where the river runs? He scoop out all that land with his hands. Like them steam shovels on the railroad. Worser."

"He must be a thing," Bennie said in a smallish voice.

They drove on. The early morning lights in the farmhouses were growing pale with the day. The farmers were out at their barns feeding their pigs and stock. The housewives were milking the cows. More than one white farmer stopped Arth, came up to his wagon, peeped at his tobacco, felt it, and bragged on it. Arth was a good farmer.

"That tobacco'll bring you around fifty cents a pound," said old Perry Hawkins with a basket of corn hung on his arm. He turned and rattled the corn at the razorback sow rooting in the edge of the potato patch.

"I sure hope it do bring that," Arth answered, cracking his whip.

"The best tobacco I've seen," old Perry called over his shoulder. "Don't let that boy freeze up there in that wind!"

"I won't, suh." Arth drove on, his heart full of warmth and happiness. Folks were good to him. The white folks were good. They always spoke kind to him. Some colored people didn't like white folks. But they were all right. They didn't bother him. He wasn't afraid to be around the sheriffs and police in town. He'd never done anything mean. He didn't mind their billies nor their buttons and badges. Some black folks couldn't stand 'em, couldn't stand to be around 'em. It made them uneasy.

The sale would be at nine o'clock and long before that time Arth and Bennie had reached the town and driven their load into the warehouse. All was turmoil and bustle there. Lucy and Mag, the two mules, tried to play skittish at the trundling baskets and tobacco trucks. When the tobacco had been un-loaded and weighed—it gained several pounds, and that was good—Arth and Bennie drove out of the warehouse into a back lot where they hitched the team to a fence. It was a few minutes before the sale, and Arth took Bennie into a rundown fruit store, where a red-hot heater was going and several men standing around, and bought him a coca-cola. The men were all white, and Arth and Bennie stood away from the stove at a respectful distance. But they didn't mind that either. That's the way things were. The fire was going strong and they soon were warm a-plenty. Presently a bell rang at the warehouse and they all hurried to the sale.

The warehouseman, a towering red-faced man, was stand-ing among a group of farmers, addressing them. "Boys," he said, "this is the old warehouse Number Four, where you get the best prices—the best prices. If anybody," he shouted, "don't like what his tobacco brings today, just let me know!" Arth, holding little Bennie by the hand, drew up closer, listening.

"That's the way to talk, ain't it?" he said, squeezing Bennie's hand. "It sound good."

"Yes, suh," Bennie answered, watching the warehouseman with open mouth.

"Now, gentlemen!" the red-faced man shouted again, "we got the best buyers here on the market! Ain't no pinhookers here—no pinhookers!" And he gestured toward three or four men in their shirt sleeves and vests over to one side who were chewing cigar stubs and talking to two young clerklike fellows carrying pencils and pads. "And this here auctioneer, Sim Howington, the best there is between the Pee Dee and the Roanoke. The best there is anywhere for that matter!" He slapped a heavy beefy fellow on the shoulder—a big stodgy squab of a man, wearing a yellow cap, a flashy suit, and with a carnation in his buttonhole.

"I am that," the auctioneer allowed, all set and ready to go and drawing his mouth down to one side until his jaw teeth showed.

"Everybody this way!" the warehouseman roared, leading the crowd over to the first row of laid-out tobacco. "All right, go to it, Sim." And he retired. Sim crawled heavily up on the first pile of tobacco, grinding the yellow silken leaves with huge uncharitable feet.

"Lord, he sure do treat it rough," Arth breathed to himself.

"Now, ladies and gentlemen—gentlemen," he said gently to the crowd of upturned faces, "I'm here to sell this tobacco, and I'm going to sell it. I want you fellows," as he turned to four or five shirt-sleeved buyers, "hah—you Liggett and Myers, you American Tobacco Company, you R. J. Reynolds—I want you folks to speak up and pay the top notch today as usual. These people here have worked hard to grow this golden weed and they don't want to give it away. No siree, they want money for it, good cash money." His voice grew suddenly louder and businesslike. "Hah—look outside, the sun is shining. It's a fair day. Look all around inside. Look at the tobacco—Lord, look at it. Hah—ain't it a sight! You heard me. Here are the farmers, depending on you gentlemen to give 'em their money's worth. The wife needs new clothes, the children got to be fixed for school. The old Ford and the Chevrolet need more gas, need new tires."

"He can speak better'n the governor of the state," Arth whispered to Bennie. "I heard that man onct."

His words were lost, for now the auctioneer let out a loud yell, as he suddenly threw up his hands, whirled about, and fixed each buyer with his eye. "What do you gimme, what do you gimme? What do you say—?" His tongue began to roll in his mouth like the clapper in a cowbell. "And-a-la, and-a-la. And-a-la-la-la-la." His voice rose and sank, ran up and down the scale, and bounded along. Bennie watched him fascinated. So did Arth. The buyers soused their hands into the bundles, felt them, smelled them, watching out for mold and worm marks, some shaking their heads, some nodding. "And what do you gimme? —Ah-la-la-la," sang the auctioneer.

"Twenty-two," one of the buyers barked.

"Twenty-two! —Er—er—ah. Twenty-three!" he bellowed as he caught the wink of another buyer's eye. Once more he reached out his hands and pleaded with them to raise him another cent. "Who'll make it twenty-four—who'll make it twenty-four?—Ooh—roo-roo—ooh! Twenty-four, twenty-four— who'll say twenty-four?" The buyers, without answering him, moved on to the next pile with impassive faces. The clerks with their pads came behind, marked on a card the initial of the buyer at twenty-three cents, and stuck it in the pile of tobacco sold. The auctioneer was on top of the second pile, now in full steam. It was sold. Nineteen cents. Down the line he moved, roaring like a man out of the asylum. He sang, he cried, he wrung his hands. He beat the air. His voice rose to a shriek, sank to a low grumble. And all the while his calm hawklike eye waited to flash upon each gesture or wink that denoted a bid. And so it went from shining row to shining row that stretched across the acre of warehouse floor. The farmers followed him up, examining the price tag of each pile and commenting upon the quality and the price. They laughed and joked. Their faces were wreathed in smiles. "Such prices!"

Arth and Bennie moved ahead and stood by their pile, which was near the middle of the house, waiting as the auctioneer and buyers approached. Now they are only five piles away, now four, now three. Arth held little Bennie's hand so tight that he cried out, "Pappy, you a-hurting of me!" Now they're on the pile next to his. It was good-looking stuff. " 'Bout good as mine," Arth whispered. It was knocked down at forty cents. The auctioneer stepped plumb in the middle of Arth's pile, and the poor fellow winced under his clothes. "Oh, Lord, he's rough!" he moaned softly.

"Forty and a forty and a forty," he sang. The cold sweat broke out on Arth's forehead.

"Jesus, gimme more'n that," Arth muttered. The auctioneer looked across at him with a wide genial leer. A buyer raised his finger. "Forty-five, forty-five—aley, aley, aley—eep, eep, eep—thry-oop, thru-oop, thru-oop. Forty and a five, and a five. Who'll gimme fifty?" Arth's knees were weak as another buyer raised his finger. And he heard the auctioneer say, "Fifty, fifty—bid up, bid up. La-la-la-lala," he sang. "Help him pay off the mortgage," cried Sim. "Save the homestead. Get him a set of new gold teeth. Who'll gimme fifty-five, fifty-five? And a five, and a five?" He begged, he stretched out his hands. But the buyers' faces grew impassive, dismissive. They were gone to the next pile. Arth saw the clerk write on a card and place it in the tobacco. He had heard them say fifty. "See what it brung, son," he said to Bennie.

"Fifty cents," Bennie held up the card. He was smart and could already read figures right off from his one year of schooling.

Now the Negro helpers were busy everywhere with their baskets and floor trucks, hauling away the tobacco as fast as it was sold. Arth stood by as they piled his on and carried it out through the door and dumped it on the waiting motor trucks to be hauled to the grading and storing plant. It gave him a pang to see it go. It was the best tobacco he'd ever raised, yellow as gold and smelling so sweetly it made your mouth water to eat it.

He and Bennie returned to the store and bought a can of sardines and a box of crackers. They sat on the wagon seat in the warm sunshine and ate while Lucy and Mag were chewing their fodder. Afterwards Arth went into the warehouse and stood by the bookkeeper's window. He gave his name and lot number. The bookkeeper turned away and began searching through a pile of slips. On to the bottom he went and turned over the last one. Arth's heart stood still. This selling and buying was so mysterious, he couldn't understand it all. Sure, some day something would happen and he wouldn't get his money. Be just like it to happen today. But then the man turned away to another pile of slips, began turning them over, stopped, and drew out one. He opened a big checkbook, wrote in it—Arth heard the sweet sound of the pen scratching along—tore out the check and handed it through the window to him. "Six hundred and thirty-seven dollars and a half, with floor charges deducted," the man said. Arth held the precious bit of paper in his hand and stared at it.

"Get out the way, nigger—you paralyzed?" a hoarse voice snapped, and a little hoop-legged white tenant farmer with dancing eyes and a ragged smile pushed up to the window. Arth started and jumped away, snatching off his hat and bowing in a shower of instinctive apologies.

"Sixty-one dollars," he heard the bookkeeper say to the fellow as he handed another check through the window. Arth stood staring at the floor, a dull disconsolate ache somewhere in his breast. After a moment he slowly put on his hat.

Oh, well, it didn't matter. He could beat 'em raising 'bacco. And Bennie was—"That's a sharp boy." He'd be smart as any of 'em. He Arth would beat 'em at farming and Bennie would beat 'em at books. You watch him. Then making a little awkward gesture with his hands as if dismissing such things, he went out to the wagon and hitched up the mules. His eyes were laughing again now as he helped Bennie to the seat and put the reins in his hands.

"I'm gonna let you drive home, son, all by yourself."

"Me? Lordy!" Bennie giggled in a flood of joy, reaching for the whip.

"You drive on there into that street, and right on down it into the road. And that leads you straight home. I be home afterwhile. Now ne' mind what I'm gonna do—you just go on!!"

Bennie cracked his whip and finally urged the dogged Lucy and Mag into a walk. Arth stood in the edge of the street and watched him until he had disappeared down the road beyond. "Them mules harmless as doves," he said. "They take him straight home. Lord, that boy sets up straight as a man. Ain't he something!" Then he went to the bank and cashed his check. Six hundred dollars and nearly fifty more, as he raked it from the till. It made a big bulge in his trousers pocket. As he came out of the bank, he could see down the street a block away a sign. "Ford Dealer," it said. He strode boldly down there and went in. A man was pottering about with greasy overalls on and a wrench in his hands.

"What you want?" he said shortly. Arth's eyes had already fastened on a gleaming new runabout.

"I wanter look at a new Ford."

"Mr. Edwards!" the greasy man shouted, eyeing Arth's old overcoat pinned with a peg.

Out of the caged-in office stepped a spry young fellow with a red necktie and a rakish derby hat. "What do you want?"

"I'd like to look at some Fords, suh."

He too eyed him narrowly. "All right," he snapped. "What sort you want?"

"I want that two-passenger there."

"That's six hundred and nineteen dollars. I've got some used ones at the back. Come on, I'll show you."

"I'll take this 'un, I believe," said Arth. He went around it, looked at it, feeling the tires, pulling shyly at the fenders to see if they rattled, trying in vain to look unconcerned. "Yessuh, I'll take it," he concluded.

"Know how to drive?"

"Yes suh, a little bit. Mr. Ed Roberts let me drive his one day. He's got a Ford." It was easier to talk now. "Mebbe you know him."

"I don't know him. All right, it's yours for the money." Arth counted out the bills.

"Hey, Fred," the man called. "Take him out up the road and give him a lesson or two!" The fellow in overalls got into the car, backed it from the shed, and drove out of town with Arth beside him. On the country road he showed him how to shift gears, start and stop, told him about oil and gas and water. In an hour or so Arth was able to handle it himself and drove it back to town. "You learn fast," said Fred drily.

"Thanky suh," said Arth humbly and pleased.

The young man with the red necktie and derby had the title papers all drawn up and gave them to him in an envelope.

"How about the licenses?"

"Yeh, you'll have to have a license. You can get it in Raleigh."

"Reckon it'll be all right for me to drive home without 'em and get 'em—well, about Monday?"

"I'll fix you a card." He got a piece of cardboard and with a heavy pencil wrote on it, "license applied for," and fastened it on the holder behind.

Fred helped him drive out to the edge of town, and there left him. Arth went skimming along the flat dirt road, as light as a bird. The smell of the new motor and upholstery sweetly filled his nostrils. And the wide fields and woods slipping by on either side warmed him and joyed his heart. Through the hollows, over the bridges and up the hills he chugged. When he came into the precincts of his own neighborhood, a wide embarrassed grin sat upon his face. Try as he would he couldn't keep it off. Neighbors came out and stared at him as he passed, some of them throwing sharp envious looks at him and his new turnout, and others frankly pleased at his pleasure and pride.

Near dusk he drove up the lane that led to his cabin and stopped. Yeh, Bennie was back. There was the wagon, and mules were in the lot with their heads hung over the gate, already looking curiously and somewhat supiciously at the new contraption. Ada and Bennie peered out through the door and drew timidly back. Her first thought was that the officers—as they called the sheriff and his deputies—had come upon them. She always thought of officers, for her father had once been arrested for helping at a whiskey still in Hector's Creek Swamp. Arth called her to come out. And she and Bennie and the two little ones finally came and stood around him and the Ford, dumb with wonder.

"That's my surprise," Arth chuckled, feeling the radiator to see if it was too hot. "That baby sure can cover ground."

"I declare—I declare!" was all Ada could say as she walked around and around. And when Arth blew the horn, the little children squealed and clung to her skirts terrified.

"Crawl in, everybody," he said, "and I'll take you down the road and back." After much arguing he got them all crowded in. He backed out of the yard and started off. Ada sat tightly gripping the side of the door. And only when they had returned did she find her voice.

"Ain't it queer how it go along with nothing to pull it?"

"Yeh, she got a little horsepower under her hood," Arth chortled gleefully.

That night the old wagon stood out in the weather, and the new Ford had its place under the shelter. Next day they drove below Dunn to see Aunt Sarah Tart and the folks. And how their relatives' eyes did shine! In the afternoon Arth took the Tart girls, gawky and giggling, around through the countryside. Aunt Sarah once had hoped that her ebony black eldest daughter, Ludie, a sprawling girl with front teeth protruding like a squirrel's, would get Arth. And things were going along pretty well until Arth had met the shy, soft-voiced Ada at an ice cream supper.

Today Aunt Sarah stayed at home and said to Ada, "You sure hit it right when you married Arth. You ought to be thankful for such a man."

"I'm satisfied," Ada answered with gentle but deep confirmation.

"Yeah, you two sure doing well," she said affectionately. "Bygones were bygones and she had no hard feelings. Her gals were not much to look at and the men didn't take to them. But that night she told the girls that Arth was getting biggety and running through with his substance.

By nightfall he and his family were at home again. Many a time on the way, Ada, as if trying to placate her sense of economy within, kept saying joyously, "We can't afford no car, Arth, we can't afford it."

"Sure we can. We don't owe nobody, we got money. Two bales of cotton left. Might's well have a little fun. Might's well, hadn't we?"

"Yeh, but we oughter be laying up for little Bennie's schooling."

"Hunh," Arth snorted, "I'll have plenty money for that. I done been a-figgering. Ain't I got a 'greement with Mr. Roberts to farm his land on the fourth for the next five years? No by the halves with me, no suh. Three or four more good crop seasons and we'll have enough laid up. And this Ford'll last us ten year with good care. And, honey, it don't take much to run it." He was in earnest now. "It don't take much. And it ain't like a mule. It don't eat when it ain't working." He laughed joyously.

The next day was Sunday, and as usual, they slept late. When they had had breakfast they washed and purtied the children, dressed them out, and went to church. As they drove into the churchyard, there was a great craning of necks out of the windows and whispering from the assembled black congregation. Several old rail-like horses and mules tied to the trees about the church snorted and shied around violently at the car, and Arth had to stop in the broomstraw by the edge of the grove to keep them from breaking loose from their rot-eaten halters and bridles.

All during the sermon he kept cutting his eye out of the window to see that everything was safe. He almost rose out of his seat when he saw two prowling boys get up in the Ford and sit down. When the collection came around he thought he detected a look of admiration and respect in the eyes of the black deacon. And thereupon he laid a one dollar bill in the plate. Ada nudged him in alarm, but he whispered reassuringly to her, "This one time. Us can spare it." After the service an admiring crowd gathered around the car. Arth was the first Negro in the whole community to own one and they paid him proper attention.

When they had returned home and eaten a hasty dinner, they decided to drive out toward Sanford to see Uncle Reuben and Aunt Mary. On the road they ran out of gas. Arth had forgotten all about the gas. Ada and the children waited, hours it seemed, while he walked two miles to a filling station and got some in an oil can. Babe Teensy howled pitifully all the while and the crackers in the old satchel didn't seem to satisfy her. Sissy and Bennie began to fight over the horn which they kept blowing now and then in spite of their mother. In the scuffle, Sissy fell out, bounded on the running board, and rolled into the ditch. Such a howl she raised! Ada lost her temper and gave Bennie a cuff on the ear, and all three children set up loud wails. White people passed in their cars now and then, looked at them coldly and apathetically through the swirling dust. A little white boy on the back seat of his father's big car ran out his tongue and thumbed his nose as they whizzed past. "Oh, I do wish we were slam home again, I do," Ada complained fretfully. After an hour or more, Arth showed up with the gas, and they drove on again.

But it was too late to go to Uncle Reuben and Aunt Mary's now. The sun was in the tops of the trees, and the children were growing hungrier and more fretful every minute. When they got to Mamers and a wide place in the road, they turned around and went home.

But Arth had not done enough riding yet, and after supper he told Ada he was going to the night service at the church. And off he went, and what a wonder it was to turn on the headlights and see the road clear before him!

He took his place timidly in the back of the church and near a window where he could keep a watch on his car outside. But lo and behold, the deacon came around and asked him to come up and sit at the front in the amen corner. "Yessuh, Brother Arth," said the smiling deacon, "a man of yo' substance and free kind soul—us needs you to be nigh unto the altar."

And with a feeling of keen elation Arth went along down the aisle under three-score pairs of sharp inquisitive eyes. The sermon was about foreign missions and the preacher laid it on thick. He drew ghastly, heart-wringing pictures of the poor and destitute, starving in Asia. "Five dollar'll keep a child alive with feed and clothing for a whole month," he told them, and Arth felt the preacher's eye upon him. So when the plate came around, he laid a crumpled bill in it. And the preacher stepped down from the rostrum and shook his hand.

"This brother's religion is where his pocketbook is, and that's right." There was a low titter somewhere in the audience and Arth felt worried. He didn't like that. "Mebbe I done gone and overdone it," he thought to himself. "But them poor pitiful Himdoo chillun. It'll help 'em and I can spare it just this once time." But he wouldn't tell Ada. He kept thinking about his Ford and as soon as the service broke, he hurried to the tree where he had left it parked.

But nothing was there. He stood still and stared before him a long while, paralyzed with fear. Then he started and slapped himself. "Sure, this ain't the tree I left it at." He saw the top of another tree nearby, between him and the stars. He walked over to it. But old Josh Turner's mule was tied there, and was rubbing his neck against the tree and letting out foul gruntings and little hisses of sound like escaping steam. Then Arth acted like a wild man. He went running around the churchyard from tree to tree, and into every dark corner. He fell over wagon shafts. He ran into a stump, he snagged his face on a low-hanging limb. His voice broke the night in a loud cry.

"Somebody done stole my new Ford!"

The people came pouring out of the church and the men and boys struck matches and went about searching with him, looking behind trees, the well curb, and bushes as if it were a toy thing now the size of your hand. The preacher himself unhooked the oil lamp from above the pulpit and came out to aid.

"How did they get it away from here?" Arth moaned. "I didn't hear 'em start it up."

"They must-a pushed it down the hill into the big road," somebody answered. And with the lamp they went down the slope. Sure enough, there were the tracks of the tires, crossing a little sandy drain ditch by the shoulder of the macadam highway. From here on there was no sign and couldn't be. Arth sat down on the bankside and wept like a child. Then a terrible sound smote on his ear. Somebody was laughing. Then another, then another.

He sprang furiously to his feet and shook his fists at the evil-minded congregation. Then wheeling around, he went running down the road as if the dogs were after him. But he didn't dare go home. What would Ada say? "Oh, I can't tell her about it, I just can't do it." He looked around at the sky as if seeking help therefrom. His body was streaming with sweat and the blood pumping chokingly in his neck, for he had run a solid mile. By the edge of the road he got down on his knees and reached his hands toward the network of stars in the sky.

"Jesus," he cried, "my Jesus, help me get my new car back!"

The prayer comforted him somewhat and when he rose up he saw across the valley the lights of the village of Lillington where the sheriff lived. It was four miles there but he would go. That man would help him. The officers of the law could get it back. And again he set off running.

An hour later, wet as if he had swum the river, he staggered up the main street of the little town. The sheriff lived in a red-brick dwelling near the courthouse. He went there, but all was dark. He didn't know what to do. He walked up and down the street, thinking, filled with anguish. Oh, if he could just go up and knock on the door. But he couldn't, he was afraid. Now a white man could do it, he'd not be afraid. In his turmoiling thoughts there was a great vast feeling of loneliness, an ache, as if something deeper and more significant than the lost Ford were wrong with the world. He couldn't put it into words. He didn't know what it was. But something was wrong way deep down. He sat down on a stone under the shadow of a tree and leaned his head on his hands, his mind a great dark blank of sorrow. He must have fallen into some kind of sleep for the first thing he knew a rough hand gripped him in the collar.

"What you doing here?" a voice said. He sprang up and saw the badge of Mr. Gordon Overby, the night cop, gleaming in the starlight. And the cop's hand was resting on the pistol butt in his belt.

"I wanter see the shurff," Arth stuttered.

"Unh-hunh, and what for this time of night?"

"Somebody stole my new Ford, Mr. Overby, stole it whilst I was in the church. I wanter see the shurff."

"Lordy mercy, you can't get him up now. It's one o'clock in the morning."

"I wanter see the shurff," he kept saying.

"I didn't know it was you, Arth, setting here. Tell me about it," said the kindhearted policeman.

"That's just it, Mr. Overby. Somebody made off with it whilst I was at the preaching."

"What was your license number?"

A dull chill struck Arth to the bone. He thought a long while. Then he came out manfully, "I didn't have no license, but—" he interposed quickly—"I was gonna get 'em in Raleigh tomorrow. That man said I could wait till Monday. I had a pasteboard he put on it."

"Well, I don't reckon there's much harm in driving awhile with no number. I tell you what you do. You come over in the morning and see the sheriff. Tell him what kind of a car it was—"

"It was a new little runabout, right new."

"—Describe it to him, and maybe he can do something. But I don't believe he can, Arth, for there's so many Fords in the country. They'll file the number off the engine. Oh, they're sharp these days. Well, it sure is bad luck. I got to go now, and check around the oil mill." He turned and went away.

Arth started his long journey home. His stiff brogan shoes had already blistered his heels. The ground was cold but he took them off when he got out of town and went along barefooted. Near day he reached his cabin in the fields, and every bone in his body ached like a sore tooth. He tried to creep into the bed without waking Ada, but when he lay down she sprang up in a fright and threw her arms tight around his neck.

"Oh, where you been all this long time, honey?" she whimpered. "Where you been? You done 'bout scared me slam to death. You ain't been in a wreck have you?"

"No, everything's all right. I stayed down in the church talking to some fellows." And then he spoke up quickly, "Like a fool I run out of gas again." He had planned his story. His voice was rough and abrupt.

"What time is it?" she murmured after a little silence, laying her head back on the pillow.

"About midnight." She turned over and settled herself for sleep. And then the big Dominicker rooster in the tree outside flapped his wings and gave two loud fool crows.

"Ain't it about day?" she said. "Hear that rooster crowing?"

"Oh, they begin to crow all through the night when it gets on toward Christmas. That's honoring Jesus, they say," he answered.

Presently she was asleep, or seemed to Arth to be. When the day was breaking in the room he got up softly and dressed again. "I got to go to Raleigh and get my license today, honey," he said, bending over the bed. She stirred sleepily. "You sleep on. I be back," and he went out of the house, hitched Lucy to the old buggy and drove away.

He finally saw Sheriff MacDonald and told him his story. But the sheriff held out little hope for finding the car.

"I'll do what I can though," he said.

At noon Arth was back home and confessed it all to Ada. He had thought it over. It was best to. She'd find it out.

She heard him through with horror-stricken face and, foreseeing a storm of tears, he got his tow sack and went out into the cold fields where the wind was blowing and began picking his late scattering cotton. He heard the cars going along the highway every now and then. Soon he left the field, went down there, and sat on the bankside and watched. Presently his heart leapt up in his mouth as he saw a new Ford runabout coming up the road. It was his car. It swept by him in a cloud of dust, and he waved frantically after it. It was his all right, tires, windshield, radiator, top, and all. He couldn't tell who was driving it—some white boy. He sat down again in despair. Other cars came by and presently another runabout, just like his. During the rest of the afternoon a half-dozen new runabouts passed that way. And he soon grew hopeless.

"There ain't no use trying to find it, not a bit. All the white folks got Fords. Plenty of 'em like mine," he said.

Near dusk he returned to the house. Ada went about preparing supper, tight-lipped and hollow-eyed. He could see she'd been crying and so had little Bennie. And after supper she broke into a flood of tears and abuse. She'd told him how it would be. They couldn't afford no car. It was foolish, foolish. They'd die in the poorhouse. And then Arth, nervous and harassed beyond endurance, flew into a rage and hit her in the face. He cursed his way out of the house and went into the fields.

For an hour or more he walked up and down there by the woods, nursing the bitterness in his heart and thinking things over. He looked up at the stars and began to think about God and how his power was over everything. Yes, that God was a good God and had his eye on man, had his eye of judgment on him. He grew sorry. A wave of contrition came over him and the ache around his heart was unbearable. His lips trembled and he fell to weeping. He couldn't stand to think of Ada crying, and the look in her eyes, and the way poor suffering silent Bennie looked at him. And the two babies squalling too.

"Oh Lord, what've I gone and done?" he moaned. Flinging his arms savagely about him, he let out another oath. "Damn the new Ford, damn it to hell! What do I care about it? It ain't nothing. It can't feel. It don't mind what happens to it. Ada's the one—"

He hurried to the house, stumbled in, and flung his arms around her. "Honey, honey," he wept, burying his face on her breast. "I can't stand it, I done you mean. I can't stand it." He sat down with her in his lap and they rocked and wept in each other's tight embrace. Ada sat up and smiled at him through her tears.

"I don't care about that Ford," she murmured. "Let it go, let it go forever!"

"I don't either," he answered. "Let it go, let it go forever!" And he kissed her and kissed her.